NIGHT
OF
THE WILDING

STORM MOON SHIFTERS &
MOONFELL WITCHES NOVELLA

TJ GREEN

Night of the Wilding

Mountolive Publishing

Copyright © 2025 by TJ Green

ISBN Paperback 978-1-991313-39-3

ISBN Hardback 978-1-991313-40-9

www.happenstancebookshop.com

www.tjgreenauthor.com

Contents

One

There was only a razor-thin crescent of moon visible as Maverick Hale, alpha of the Storm Moon Pack and owner of Storm Moon, his club in Wimbledon, London, unleashed his wolf in the enormous grounds of Richmond Park.

He was accompanied by a select number of his pack members: Domino, his female Head of Security; Arlo, his Pack Second who managed the club; and Vlad, the club's Deputy Manager. They were his inner circle, privy to the secrets and issues that he kept from the rest of the wolf-shifters. There were others in that select group, such as Grey, the human Deputy Head of Security, and Jet, his human spy, but they weren't part of the hunt that night.

It was mid-June and hot, and London felt unsettled, as if something lurked beneath the blazing sun. The glare that daylight brought was almost too bright. It slanted into every corner, and the heat had made the ground hard and dry, and the grass brown. Dust rose around his pounding paws as he raced through the grounds, his three companions spread around him. It felt good to cut loose at night, and even better that it was just past the new moon. Darkness was welcome.

Without warning, half a dozen rabbits bolted into view, white tails bobbing as they bounded across the field, and rather than set off in pursuit, he waited, senses alert for what might have disturbed them. Even with his excellent night vision and acute sense of smell, he sensed nothing untoward, yet they raced away as if spooked by something. *Maybe it was him they sensed.* He was a predator after all, and as he wasn't hunting, hadn't bothered to disguise his approach.

And then a screech sundered the air, and a huge owl soared overhead, talons outstretched. Spotting Maverick, it swooped and headed directly for him. Even as Maverick sensed that something was wrong, because owls in general did not attack wolves, he still responded as his instincts demanded. He snarled, back legs bunching beneath him, ready to spring at the threat.

It was a Tawny Owl, larger than most, and its amber eyes blazed with a fiery orange light, much as Maverick's probably were. They gleamed gold when threatened, and although an owl wasn't really a threat to a creature of his size and speed, the fact that it was being blatantly aggressive was enough to provoke a reaction. As he leaped towards it, the owl turned swiftly, avoiding his snapping jaws, and its claws raked through the thick fur on his shoulder blade before rising on powerful wings and wheeling away.

Maverick landed softly on his paws, cursing his clumsiness. The bird was swifter and more agile than he had expected for such a large creature. *And that's why wolves don't chase birds. Idiot.* A wave of dizziness swept over him, and he slumped to the ground, shifting quickly back to human. The dry grass scratched his bare skin, and he barely had time to register that he'd shifted without really intending to, when Domino raced to his side and shifted, too.

"Are you all right, Mav? I saw the owl attack you." Her long, dark hair fell over her face as she crouched to inspect his wounded right shoulder. "Claw marks, but they're not deep."

"They sting like a bitch, though." He twisted to look at them. "They don't look too bad."

Domino inhaled deeply, and an odd expression swept over her face. "You smell different. What's going on?"

Maverick's hand flew to his shoulder, coming away sticky with his blood. He sniffed tentatively. "Can you smell poison? I must admit, I feel...odd." He shook off his irrational fear. "It was just an owl. I can't be poisoned. I'll sleep in my wolf tonight. It will pass." Shifters were preternaturally strong, and healed quicker than humans, especially if they stayed in their primal form. His gaze swept his surroundings, but the owl had disappeared, and so had the rabbits. In a few seconds, though, Vlad and Arlo loped towards him, shifting to human, too.

"We saw what happened," Arlo said. "Tried to follow it, but it vanished too quickly. Somewhere over Two Storm Wood. Any idea why it..." And then he stopped speaking, eyes darting to Domino and Vlad before settling on Maverick again. Arlo was his best friend, who he'd known for years. He was mixed race, with a Jamaican dad and English mom. He was normally laid back and easy-going, but his face was now creased with fear. "Where's your wolf, Mav?"

"Where it always is, you twit."

"No, it's not. I can't sense him."

Maverick could always feel his wolf. It was a part of him. The wild nature at his very core. It gave him superior strength, speed, an excellent sense of smell, and acute night vision. It also made his human side stronger. All wolf-shifters were superior to humans in every way. And as the alpha, he was quicker and stronger than his pack, but he kept his natural aggression tightly leashed. He wasn't a monster. Even so, his wolf lurked close, ready to rise should he need it. He felt for it as he always did, and then realised why he felt so odd.

It wasn't there.

"What the fuck?" Maverick's hand flew to his chest, as if he could feel it just under his skin, and he sought deep within himself. *Had it fled out of fear? Was it hiding in some part of himself he didn't know he had?* All stupid questions. His wolf never ran. "It must be here..." He stared at Domino and Vlad, seeking reassurance. "Can you sense it?"

Vlad shook his head, eyes darting away to take in their surroundings, as if he couldn't bear to look at him, but Domino kept her eyes firmly on Maverick. "No, I can't. It's just as Arlo said. It's missing. I knew something was different, but I was so focussed on your injury..."

Maverick felt sick again. Dizzy. *This couldn't be happening. He was the alpha. A born shifter. You couldn't lose your wolf...right?* "It can't have just gone!" His panic rose and his heart pounded.

Domino turned to Arlo. "Arlo, our wolves don't just vanish, and owls don't normally attack us, yet that owl attacked Maverick. Maybe it had poison on its talons."

"That suppress our wolf?" He tossed his dreads in derision. "It's not suppressed, Dom. It's *gone*. And I don't smell poison. Do you?"

Maverick felt like a child while they discussed the issue as if he wasn't even there. Was this how it was now? No wolf, no opinion? *Bollocks.* He couldn't even snarl! A wolf with no bite. It just wasn't in him anymore. He felt so weak. So ineffectual. "Guys! I'm right here. I was fine, right up until I saw that owl. It must be responsible!"

He rose to his feet feeling diminished. Like half a man, even though physically he hadn't changed at all. He scanned the sky, looking for the Tawny Owl. Unfortunately, he might look the same, but his eyes weren't. Nothing was as clear as it should be. Plus, he was naked, and it was a long walk home.

"How can an owl be responsible?" Domino asked. "It doesn't make sense. Perhaps something happened to you earlier in the day?"

"It's been a regular day, Dom, until the owl encounter. As soon as it struck me, I collapsed...so rationally, it must be the owl."

Vlad finally spoke. "Maybe it wasn't an owl."

"Another shifter?" Arlo asked.

Vlad shrugged. He was a tall, blond, and blue-eyed Dane that had been recently promoted to the role, and so far he'd been loyal and reliable. "I don't know, but owls don't normally attack wolves, and they don't steal powers."

Maverick's voice rose with anger. "Whatever it is, how can it steal my wolf? It's like stealing my soul!" He sighed when no one answered. "Raise the pack. Have them come out here and hunt that thing. It's still out there somewhere."

"Are you insane?" Arlo said, incredulous. "Let the entire pack know you've lost your wolf? You'll be challenged, and you'll lose. We can't tell anyone. Understood?" He stared at Vlad. "Vlad?"

He nodded. "Of course. It would be a disaster. But what if we're attacked? This could happen to any of us."

"It might only be temporary," Domino reasoned.

"We don't know that," Vlad pointed out. "It could be forever!"

Dizziness swept over Maverick again. He couldn't lose his wolf forever. He'd lose who he was. His place in the pack. Maybe even his life. He'd made enemies. *If the wrong people found out he was weak...* "I need to get home." Home was his luxurious flat above Storm Moon.

"No!" Arlo shook his head. "That's the last place you should be. Other pack members can find you there and detect the loss. And you can't go back with me. Jax would find out." Jax was another shifter, and Arlo's flatmate.

"Or me," Vlad said. "Mads would know. I know he's my brother, but..." He trailed off, eyes full of doubt, and Maverick understood why. Mads had struggled with Vlad's promotion, but would he really challenge Maverick? He prided himself on being a popular alpha, but with wolves that only went so far.

"Moonfell," Domino said decisively. "It's the only safe place you can go. The witches have no interest in the pack beyond helping us. They will not challenge you. They can help, and right now, we need all the help we can get."

'I don't need minders," Maverick said, glaring at his companions. "I need my wolf back."

"We three will investigate that," she said, clearly ignoring his doubts. "And I'll involve Grey. Maybe Jet, too. We'll go from there." Grey was ex-military, and always useful in a crisis. Domino squared her shoulders. "Apart from those two, we say nothing to anyone, and finding out about that damn owl is our number one priority. Is that okay, Maverick?"

Maverick hadn't felt vulnerable for years. Not since his parents died. But right now, with three aggressive wolves looking at him, wolves who knew he couldn't fight properly, he felt his fear rising but immediately squashed it. They must not sense that. No matter if they were his friends. They were still wolves. He nodded, needing to exert his alpha dominance now more than ever. "Yes, all great suggestions. Thanks, Domino. I'll head to Moonfell now, but keep me updated."

"I'll escort you, that's my job. You two," she glanced to Arlo and Vlad, "start hunting—but be careful. I'll join you when Maverick is safe."

Two

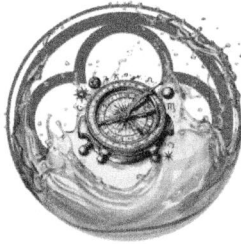

M organa Cornelius, one of the three resident witches of Moonfell, pulled several ancient grimoires from the shelves in their enormous library and arranged them on one of the wooden tables situated under an open window that overlooked the inner courtyard.

They had hundreds of grimoires, all written by the many witches that had lived in Moonfell over the centuries, or had their life's work returned there after death. Some grimoires were slim volumes that were more like personal diaries with spells throughout, while others were thick, heavy tomes filled with arcane knowledge. Their ancestors had many different skills, much like the present coven, but Morgana was specifically interested in grimoires that mentioned transfiguration. Somewhere in these pages might be the answer to their present dilemma: Maverick's missing wolf.

He had arrived in the early hours of the morning with Domino, who looked just as worried as Maverick. They all knew that the implications were huge. If they couldn't find Maverick's wolf, not only his life would be turned upside down. The entire Storm Moon Pack would be in a state of disarray, too. Packs needed stability and strong leadership, or violence could erupt. Plus, Morgana had personal reasons for wanting to help him. Not only was he her friend, but Maverick wasn't your typical alpha. He might swagger, but he wasn't a bully or a misogynist, and she liked how the pack behaved under his leadership.

"Well?" Birdie asked, bustling across the room, her Indian cotton dress fluttering around her ankles. "Any solutions yet?"

"Good grief! Give me a chance. It took a while to narrow these down." Morgana's hand swept over the collection in front of her.

Birdie was the High Priestess of the coven, and Morgana's grandmother. She was an imperious witch in her eighties, who now looked like she was in her sixties, thanks to the Goddess who had gifted her some of her years back several months before. She was also the oldest member of their coven. The third witch who lived permanently at Moonfell was Odette, Morgana's cousin, who at thirty-one was twelve years younger than Morgana.

Birdie grimaced. "Is that all there is? I had hoped there'd be more."

Morgana pointed across the library to the remaining golden orbs bobbing by some leather-bound volumes. "Other books my spell identified that may be of use."

"Still not that many, really," she said, walking over to collect them. "I suppose it's not a common issue."

"What? Transfiguration, or the stealing of one's inner animal?'

"The latter—I hope."

"How is Maverick this morning?" Morgana asked, flicking open the first grimoire and settling into a chair.

"Terrible. I've never seen him so down. He can't even muster the energy to be furious. It's really quite terrifying." Birdie tucked an errant lock of white hair behind her ear, eyes speculative. "It's as if part of his personality has been stolen, too."

Morgana tried to keep her impatience from her voice. "His identity, certainly. He *is* his wolf! They are bound, which makes me think whoever has stolen it has very powerful magic. What has happened shouldn't be possible. At least not with one touch! It should take hours of spellcasting to do such a thing." She considered the pages full of scrawled spells in front of her. It would take all day to review them all, and that was just with skim-reading. "Birdie, even if we find spells that could do such a thing, it doesn't tell us how to find his wolf, or where it's stored."

Birdie snorted. "I doubt it's in a box!"

"I am well aware of that! But where could it be? And who stole it? I mean, I know it was an owl, but *who or what* is that? Is it a therian-shifter? Or a bird-shifter? Perhaps a witch?" Morgana had so many questions, it was overwhelming.

"My dear," Birdie said calmly, "that's exactly what Odette is investigating. We must wait and see what she finds. Hopefully, she can see what Maverick saw last night in that uncanny way of hers, and gain some much-needed insight. Then of course we must see if there's anything in his wound that can reveal who or where his attacker is. I'll use the sample we took when he arrived."

Morgana nodded. They had acted swiftly upon his arrival, securing a sample of tissue at the site when his wound was fresh. "I thought you were doing that now?"

"I will. I was just checking in on you first. Hopefully, you will find a spell that can return his wolf to him."

As usual, the Moonfell Coven had divided their time and skills to speed up their investigation. Time was not on their side.

Morgana took a deep, calming breath. "This whole thing has unsettled me. It seems so...*impossible*. I will sit here until I find something useful!"

"You know," Birdie mused, "I've been wondering if the thief is a familiar."

Morgana fumbled the pages in shock. "A familiar? Has Hades told you something?"

"Unfortunately, not. He is as surprised as we are."

Hades was a large, grey, Savannah cat who had a long, checkered history with their house and their ancestors. Morgana tolerated him, but had long considered him to be too odd to be trusted. However, he was Birdie's familiar, not hers, and she trusted Birdie.

"Why would a familiar steal Maverick's wolf? They are creatures of spirit."

Birdie shrugged. "It's just a suggestion. I was throwing it in for consideration. Maybe it's a weak familiar who wanted a more powerful spirit."

"Hardly weak if it's stealing Maverick's wolf," Morgana muttered. "No, something else must be behind this. It might not even be malicious. Just misguided, perhaps."

Birdie cocked her head. "I doubt that. The paranormal world knows the enormous significance of this. Such events could be catastrophic. Plus, it sounds to me as if Maverick's attack was opportunistic, so there might be other random thefts. Maybe not just shifters, either. Other types of paranormal powers." Her eyes darkened as she considered the implications. "Witches' power, perhaps. A vampire's immortality. Some quality of a spirit, maybe. Clairvoyancy. Elemental magic. Telekinesis. Even demon powers could be harnessed. Maybe even the ability to straddle worlds."

Morgana frowned. "That's a huge assumption, Birdie!"

"But still possible."

Morgana gasped as another thought struck her. "One of the Nephilim is in London. Nahum. What if his wings were stolen? His power of flight? His near immortality?" Nahum was one of seven Nephilim who were all supernaturally strong with varied abilities inherited from their Fallen Angel fathers. "They are part angel, Birdie. If someone is collecting lots of paranormal powers, they will be very dangerous."

"We should warn him, and Maggie."

Maggie Milne was the Detective Inspector of the Paranormal Policing Unit in London. She was a lively, middle-aged woman who swore profusely and had cynicism burned into her soul, but she was very good at her job. "Yes, we should. But let's discuss it with Maverick first. He was very keen that we keep this information a secret."

Birdie headed for the door. "I know, but this could be the start of something, and we cannot afford to pretend otherwise, even for Maverick."

Now

DI Maggie Milne was having a bad day.

The weather had been stupidly hot for days. Abnormally hot, in fact. The heat in the city was stifling, and the streets baked under cloudless blue skies. She could feel sweat trickling down her neck, and from the unpleasant sensation of her sticky underarms, she had forgotten to wear deodorant that morning. But worse was the irritating woman called Isadora Sturnus, glaring at her across the table in the tiny interview room at the police station.

"I am serious! Last night I was attacked outside my flat as I was walking home. Some random bumped into me on the street and stole my powers. I cannot shift any more. I was assaulted! This is the end of my life!"

"You're not dead!" Maggie snapped.

"I may as well be. I'm a bird-shifter. My family are shifters. My clan are shifters. What use am I without the ability to shift?" All of a sudden, Isadora's irritation left her, and she burst into tears. "You must help me. I don't know what to do, or who to turn to. Isn't this your job?"

Maggie massaged her temples. "I manage paranormal policing crimes, yes, but this—"

"Is a bloody crime!" she said, wiping her tears away. "Someone has stolen my powers."

"Slow down. How do you know it was the 'random' who bumped into you? And random what, for fuck's sake? Man? Woman? Dog?"

Isadora looked sheepish. "I'd had a few drinks, so I'm not sure. I think it was a man, but he was sort of hunched over, with a hoodie pulled over his head. He had turned a corner before I even fully registered what was happening." She gestured to her wrist. "I was aware of his hand there. Or something... A light touch." She shuddered. "Ugh."

"So, whoever that was might not have been responsible at all! The touch might have been accidental."

"I felt immediately weak afterward. I could barely get through the door at first, and had to go straight to bed. I thought it was the alcohol, but then I woke up this morning and I *knew*." Isadora sat back in her chair, eyes fixed firmly on Maggie, tears banished as she desperately regained some measure of calm, but fear still lurked behind her sharp, blue gaze. "I still have shifter instincts, even if my bird has gone. Who else am I supposed to ask for help, DI Milne?"

Maggie had no faith that anyone who had been drinking knew anything concretely. Judgment was always impeded, and the loss might have happened in the pub. However, she felt sorry for the woman, and it *was* her job, although she thought it would be a tricky investigation. "I take it that you haven't heard of this happening before?"

"No, absolutely not. Not in any account of shifter history. Not bird-shifter history, at least. My family is devastated. We *all* need your help!"

"All right. Ask around, see if you can find out anything, and I'll make some enquiries."

Maggie had two detective sergeants, so one of them could start on this straight away. As for her own angle, she would ring her friend, Jackson Strange, who was the Deputy Director of the Paranormal Government Agency, situated in The Retreat beneath Hyde Park and Kensington Palace. They may be a small organisation, but they monitored all manner of supernatural activity and might be aware of unusual occurrences that could help her investigation.

If someone was stealing powers, though, this could get ugly.

As she left the interview room, her phone started ringing, identifying her caller as Birdie. Maggie groaned. Birdie did not make social calls, which meant something was wrong.

Fuck it.

Three

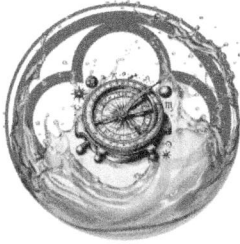

Maverick did not appreciate being the subject of Odette's intense gaze. He had witnessed her ability to see to the truth of things, her uncanny knowing that either struck unbidden or was commanded at will, but he had never imagined that he would be subjected to it.

"Please, Maverick," she said, voice gentle, but her grip on his hands like a vice, "just relax."

"Easier said than done."

"I appreciate that, but I will—hopefully—see what you saw, and know what you felt. It will help us work out who this is."

They were in the summerhouse in the west of the garden, and Odette's wild curls framed her small, heart-shaped face. As usual, she wore old jeans, an even older t-shirt covered with paint, and her feet were bare. She was delicate of build, but there was nothing else delicate about Odette. Like all the Moonfell witches, she had a core of steel. She sat opposite him, mirroring his cross-legged position, their knees touching, hands linked.

"I feel...vulnerable. I don't like it." To even confess it aloud was bad enough.

Her gaze softened. "I know, and I'm sorry. Have you slept? Because you look like shit."

"Of course I haven't fucking slept! Someone has stolen part of me. *Most* of me! I am a wolf, Odette!"

The witches had been gracious when he'd arrived in the middle of the night, concerned for his well-being. They had questioned him extensively, taken a sample from his wound before dressing it, and then given Maverick one of the guest bedrooms on the second floor. He had tried to sleep, but after tossing and turning, he extricated himself from his tangled bedsheets and headed to the window to study Moonfell's extensive grounds with its winding paths that connected lots of different garden areas. Over the previous months he had grown familiar with them, thanks to the witches allowing the pack members to exercise their wolf here in daylight. A great luxury in the city. Moonfell's garden was as mysterious as the house, possessing special magic of its own. But wards of protection kept the place safe, so that whatever had attacked him couldn't get inside. Somewhere beyond the walls, the three shifters hunted, but no one called him with updates, and exhausted, he finally managed to sleep briefly in the hours before dawn.

When he'd woken, he had discovered his own clothing and toiletries outside his room, so at least he didn't have to wear Lamorak's clothes. He was Morgana's son. But it wasn't enough to assuage the loss of his wolf. He felt hollow. Like someone had scooped out his insides.

"Maverick," Odette said, summoning his drifting attention, "I thought we'd do this in the garden because it's where you're more relaxed, so take a deep breath, enjoy the fresh air, and let me do my thing. The sooner we do this, the better."

Peevish, he asked, "So why didn't we do it when I arrived?"

"Because you were overwrought, and I was tired—a bad combination. Plus, I wanted to think about my approach. This is a spell I haven't used in a while, so bear with me."

"Fine. Go ahead."

"Good, now walk me through the event. Where you were, how you felt, and be thorough. Details are good."

Feeling idiotic, Maverick did as she asked, describing the run through Richmond Park. The freedom. The power. And then his curiosity. A strange thing happened as he talked. Time seemed to slow around him, the air feeling syrupy and thicker than usual in the heat that gripped London. He was so intent on his description, Odette's eyes holding his own, that the world beyond the summerhouse slipped away, and suddenly he was in the park again, the sky a scatter of stars above him, the beat of wings close. He flinched in panic, but she was in his head, and weirdly he still felt his hands in her slender ones.

"I'm still here," she said, voice as smooth as silk. "I see what you see. Keep going."

Now

Odette hadn't tried this spell for a long time, and wasn't sure that using it on Maverick would be wise, but she needed answers.

She'd felt a trace of guilt at not revealing exactly what the spell would do, because she honestly wasn't sure it would work at all. Maverick may not have his wolf anymore, but he was strong. Now, seeing through his eyes, she watched the rabbits bolt across the field, and felt the heat of the night. She sensed his power, too, and revelled in his raw, wolf masculinity.

It was utterly different to a witch's power, and his muscular build was completely unlike her own. She slipped inside his skin and embraced his strength. It was intoxicating. He was at one with his surroundings. Both part of it, and the master of it. All bowed to the wolf. Especially the alpha. He knew it, too, and he'd earned that respect. The world through his eyes was more intense, his depth perception impressive, but even more impressive was the tightly-reined power at his core.

The screech of the owl drew her attention upwards, and she saw what Maverick couldn't. A nimbus of power around the creature. It was not an owl at all, that was certain. As it turned and dived on Maverick, she felt its glee and saw the presence within it. Old, grasping, and utterly selfish. The rake of claws on his shoulder burned with unexpected heat, but what followed was worse. His power was decimated as his wolf was ripped from him, dragged out by the owl's claws, and the shade of it trailed behind the creature before vanishing entirely.

Odette barely had time to process it when she was swept back to the present by Maverick who slumped forward in a dead weight. "Maverick! Are you okay?"

Deep shudders wracked his body, his face buried in her lap. "I didn't expect to experience it again. It was worse than the first time, because I knew it was coming." He finally pulled himself upright, eyes fierce, although they lacked his alpha's smouldering power. "What the fuck did you do?"

"Sorry. The spell was more effective than I thought." Odette released his hands and placed hers over her heart as if to heal a wound. "I felt your loss, Maverick. It was horrible. Well, a fraction of it, perhaps. To have that power ripped from you..."

"Did you see it? Feel it happening?"

"I saw the creature drag your wolf from your body like it was nothing, and felt its loss like a blow." Maverick looked so anguished that the horror of it struck her again. "I'm so sorry. I don't know what it is yet, but I know it isn't an owl, and I also know it's very old." Part of her was still in Richmond Park at night, and she shook her head to dispel it, finally slipping back into the present again as the summer day returned. Moonfell's garden was like a balm to her senses after that. She hoped Maverick thought so, too.

Maverick's shoulder-length, dirty blond hair had fallen over his face, but he brushed it away now, his expression hardening. "You saw it take my wolf? Like it had a form?"

"Yes. Have you heard of astral projection? Spirit-walking it's also called." He nodded. "The soul has shape, and when you leave your corporeal body behind, your spirit holds its human shape. I have spirit-walked on occasions. The soul connects to the body with a silvery rope. To sever it means death. Well," she shrugged, feeling her description inadequate for such a mystical event, "that's the basic outline.

Your wolf spirit had wolf form, but there was no silvery rope connecting it to you. It was pulled from you, and the creature..." Odette hesitated, seeing it happening again. "Your wolf spirit vanished, but I think that creature absorbed it."

"I will rip it apart limb by limb. Can you find it?"

She closed her eyes, trying to see the form beyond the owl, but it was so amorphous. When she opened her eyes again, it was to find Maverick still staring at her, eyes searching her face for clues. "It was shapeless and dark, but it was very old. I sensed that much. It will be close, too. It was confident in its power, so I doubt it will flee. It will have found a place to shelter."

"But can you find it?"

She stood up, unwilling to commit. "Let's wait and see what Birdie finds out. First, I need to paint."

"Paint?"

"It often helps me visualise our problems more clearly—and by that, I mean our attacker."

If she could see it, maybe she could name it.

Four

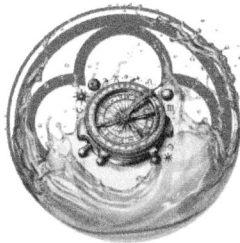

M aggie passed through the security checks in The Retreat, for once glad to be in its labyrinthine passages and out of the glaring heat of London.

The luxurious Art Nouveau décor was a reminder of the fact that it was built by Princess Louise in the early part of the 20th century. She was the fourth daughter of Queen Victoria, a fiercely independent woman who was interested in the paranormal. She created The Retreat specifically for the small government organisation, and was closely involved with its design. She had lived in Kensington Palace for years, and somewhere in these passages was a way to access the palace. No doubt it had been closed up since then. Maggie felt an affinity with the woman, if not the place. She sounded like someone she could enjoy chatting with over a few drinks in the pub. *Not that the princess would likely ever frequent a pub.*

Loud voices up ahead made Maggie quicken her step, and as she rounded a bend in the passageway, saw a cluster of figures by the analysts' office. One of them was Jackson Strange, and the other smaller man was Waylen Adams, the director of the organisation. There was someone else she couldn't see, but she recognised his voice immediately. It was JD, the immortal Director of The Orphic Guild. His peevish, abrupt tones echoed down the corridor, and she smirked. He had been engaged to oversee the science department's experiments with alchemy, but no doubt was sticking his nose into everything.

"My dear woman," he said, his sharp tone carrying easily, "you must be specific. How many incidents? How long? How far?"

A harassed-sounding young woman said, "We're collating it all now, but it seems to have erupted over a matter of hours!"

That was the new analyst, a woman called Julia, who had only been working matter of months after the previous female analyst had been killed. She shared the office with Austin, another analyst who also monitored paranormal incidents in the UK. Together, they divided the UK between them. Maggie peeked over Waylen's shoulder.

JD, dapper, white-haired, and trim, huffed. "But details are important."

Julia glared, holding her own. "I'm an analyst. I know that. It's what we do!"

Maggie nudged Jackson and pulled her tall, shaggy-haired friend away from the argument. He cared little for his appearance, and constantly mooched around in jeans, trainers, and a creased jacket that was often covered by his long trench coat. "I think you may have some answers for me after hearing all this. Problem?"

"Seems so." He rolled his eyes. "Bloody JD. He would pick this morning to come and see us. He has a knack for aggravating every situation."

"What's happened?"

"A series of paranormal attacks overnight."

Maggie frowned, ignoring the row that was erupting in the office. "I had a report this morning. A shifter who had had their shifter-animal stolen—a bird, actually. Then Birdie phoned me—Moonfell's High Priestess."

Jackson's mouth fell open in shock. "Have they had problems?"

"No, but Maverick has. Remember me mentioning him? He's the alpha wolf of the Storm Moon Pack." He nodded. "He had his wolf stolen last night, and now he's hiding out at Moonfell. If his pack finds out..." She didn't need to say more. Jackson understood the consequences.

"Herne's flaming bollocks!" Jackson sagged against the wall. "We do not need instability at Storm Moon."

"I don't need it *anywhere*! The witches will help us, and so will Domino and Arlo. I gather there is a very small number of the pack that know what has happened to Maverick, and they will keep it that way, so they'll do anything to support him. However, I need more information. What else has happened?"

"The events were picked up by the regular police force. A few people—exact numbers to be confirmed—were found unconscious on the street or in parks. They have no memory of events, but claim to have had their powers stolen. I think you'll find your sergeants will be knee-deep in reports when you leave this place."

"Shifters actually confessed to having powers to someone in the regular police force? Had they lost their marbles, too?"

"They were in shock. Early reports suggest they were confused and rambling. And they weren't just shifters, either. A witch claimed her power was stolen, too." Jackson huffed. "You can imagine the response. The regular police hate to deal with this stuff."

"You don't need to tell me. I have to put up with their nervy looks and sly fucking comments all the time. Useless bastards." Maggie had worked in their very small and under-resourced team for years, first as a detective sergeant, then the lead DI. She liked the unusual work, but it certainly wasn't for everyone, and her team kept to themselves for the most part. She leaned against the wall, hitched her bag over her shoulder, and grabbed her notebook and pen from its crowded interior. "I'll get the list from Austin and Julia, just in case some stations haven't passed everything on. Are there only reports from London?"

"So far, but this is early in our investigation."

"A specific area, then?"

"Let's ask, shall we? I arrived only minutes before you."

Waylen, mild-mannered and affable, was trying to get JD to shut up. "JD, this really isn't your concern. Perhaps you should return to the lab."

"I don't want to! This is extremely interesting. Whoever is stealing powers must be powerful, and therefore worthy of my attention. Even more interesting is what they must want these powers for."

"That makes two of us, then," Maggie said, drawing his attention.

JD turned, affronted, and then grinned. "Maggie Milne! You old fish wife! How good to see you."

"I see you're causing trouble again, you pompous popinjay," Maggie shot back, always pleased to verbally joust with JD.

His eyes gleamed. "Poisonous, hunch-backed toad."

"Thou crusty batch of nature!"

JD's mouth fell open in delight. "Madam! *Troilus and Cressida*. You outdo yourself."

Waylen groaned. "Shut up! Both of you. This is serious!"

"Why else am I here, Waylen?" Maggie asked. "I have better things to do than roaming the halls of this place. I've had one report this morning, but had no idea there had been so many other attacks. I need to narrow down the search area. This thief is clearly bold and very fucking quick."

"Or there's more than one," Jackson pointed out.

"Don't forget powerful," JD added.

Maggie turned to Austin and Julia. "Hi, guys. Suggestions, please?"

Austin answered, his Birmingham accent at odds with the assorted London ones. "As we're trying to explain, reports are coming in thick and fast, and they are all attacks that happened overnight. Most seem to be from shifters who have been targeted, but witches have had their magic stolen, too. I have a feeling that these are just the tip of the iceberg."

Maggie exchanged a worried glance with Jackson. "You're probably right. Most paranormal activity goes unreported. We all know that." The paranormal community liked to dole out their own brand of justice. The attacks could lead to hostility and fighting if the separate factions decided one of the others was responsible. "This has taken everyone by surprise, obviously," she mused. "That's why some are talking. Potentially, this has been planned for a while."

Waylen's foot tapped the floor as he considered the problem. "I agree with Jackson. It could be a group."

"Hard to know right now," she conceded. "But whoever is involved has struck quickly, and that worries me. It might mean it was a one-night event to steal as much power as they could. Were they only night-time attacks?"

The analysts scanned their data, and Julia nodded. "Looks that way."

"A nocturnal creature, perhaps?" JD asked.

Maggie shrugged. "Maybe. But what do they want all of this power for? To start a paranormal war? Because it could end up that way unless we act fast. I need a location. Can you at least give me a rough area to focus on?"

Austin nodded, turning back to his computer. "Give me one minute."

"Perhaps," JD said thoughtfully, "we are jumping to conclusions by presuming that this was planned. It could be an old creature that has recently awoken for some reason."

"Or pressed into action," Waylen suggested, "by someone else. It might be a puppet."

"I'll keep an open mind," Maggie said. "JD, we might need your alchemical weapons. This thing—or things—could be hard to fight."

"Some of them are here, so help yourself, but I suggest you also call Nahum. Does he know? A Nephilim's fighting skills are far superior to your own."

She bridled. "Thank you. I am well aware of that. He might not want to get involved. Olivia is very pregnant now." For the first time in centuries, the baby of a Nephilim was due to be born. No one knew what the outcome could be, and Nahum was twitchy.

"Really?" JD said scathingly. "I would think he'll be very happy to dispatch something that could harm his offspring, or Olivia. Depending on what our thief is looking for, they could be a valuable target."

Austin's excited tones cut into their conversation. "The attacks happened in an area to the southwest. They are randomly spaced, but even so." He turned the computer screen to show a map of London with lots of red dots. "They are on either side of the river, and encompass quite a bit of greenspace and ponds around, but there's one place central to them all. Hampton Court Palace."

Maggie headed for the door. "It's a start. Keep me updated!"

Now

Domino searched the security footage of the club area of Storm Moon that had been recorded the previous night, trying to discern any unusual behaviour while her friends discussed their options behind her.

Storm Moon had three floors. The bar on the ground floor, the club in the basement, and Maverick's flat on the first floor. The bar was too open and well-lit to allow for suspicious meetings, but the club was perfect for them. It was usually loud, due to the resident DJ and the regular bands, and there were several small rooms that allowed for discreet chats. They were in the Security Office that overlooked the club via a huge, one-way window, but it was mid-afternoon, and the club was closed.

Domino glanced over her shoulder to where Jet was talking to Grey, Vlad, and Arlo. "You spotted nothing unusual then, Jet?"

"No, sorry. Last night seemed just like any other. Lots of new faces, of course, but that's nothing new. Lots of familiar ones, too. Certainly nothing suspicious, beyond the usual gossip."

Jet was petite and dark-haired, with many tattoos and a fondness for bold makeup. Her good looks made her their perfect spy. Her official job was a member of the bar staff, but she circulated the floor regularly, talking and gathering information.

"However," she continued, "I guarantee there'll be lots of chat tonight, if Maggie is correct. Things could be tense."

Maggie had just phoned them with an update. Initially, Domino was annoyed that the witches had told Maggie about Maverick, before eventually admitting that the more help they had, the better. She had been paranoid that this was a Storm Moon-targeted attack, but the fact that lots of paranormals had been victimised made her feel slightly better.

"Let's increase security, then," Arlo said, nodding to Vlad and Grey. "We don't need fights breaking out."

The other staff would be arriving soon, so they needed to get their story straight. It had been a horrible few hours. Although she didn't want to admit it, Domino had been severely unnerved searching Richmond Park for clues to Maverick's attacker. The owl had come out of nowhere, and if Maverick couldn't stop it, neither would they. Domino did not want to lose her own wolf. The thought terrified her, even though she'd kept calm in front of the others. She suspected Arlo and Vlad were feeling the same way.

The other thing that had scared her was how hard it had been to remain submissive to Maverick. She loved him as their alpha, but her wolf—her aggressive core—had found him wanting without his wolf. Plus, she had scented his fear. She and Arlo were old friends, but Vlad might not have that degree of loyalty, and she watched him warily now as they discussed the evening ahead with the others. He seemed fine, but what if he was seizing his moment? He could kill Maverick easily when only a human. And then she'd have to kill Vlad. Thank the Gods Maverick was at Moonfell with the witches. She just wished they would call with news.

Vlad looked over at her, eyes narrowing, and abruptly left the others talking and headed to her side. "Domino, can we speak outside?"

"Is there a problem?"

"Yes." His blue eyes bore into hers, and she felt suddenly guilty. She liked Vlad. Trusted him. *Normally.*

"Fine." She left the office, leading him down the corridor to one of the small lounges where she turned to face him. He towered over her, although she was tall for a woman; but she was used to intimidating strong men. She hadn't achieved her role as Head of Security for being a wilting flower. "Go on."

"You don't trust me. I've seen you shooting me suspicious glances all morning. What have I done to deserve this? I am loyal to Maverick—and you!"

"You could barely look at him last night. It worried me."

"We're skirting around the main issue, which is that we all struggled last night. It was hard seeing him like that. I saw it in you, too, you know."

"It was a shock, but I've known him a long time."

He sneered. "You think because I'm not an old, valued friend that I'm suddenly untrustworthy? Fuck you, Domino! Maverick saved me and my brother. Restored our faith in alphas after the bastard that nearly killed us. You think I'm so shallow that I would kill him now that he's weak?"

She blinked, shocked at his candour, but rallied. "We're predators..."

"But we still have reason. I'm not a fucking traitor, Domino. Or merely an animal. I hunted with you last night, and like you, did not wish to risk my wolf, but I did it anyway." He folded his arms across his broad chest. "Do you want me to go? Take me off the case? Sack me?"

Bollocks. All of that was true. This situation was addling her judgment. "No! Of course not. I'm sorry, and I admit, I'm feeling paranoid." She slumped onto one of the soft sofas. "This is the worst thing that could happen!"

"I know! I'm terrified, and I hate to admit that." He sat opposite her, long legs stretched out as he sank into the cushions, reaching his arms across the sofa back. Wolves seemed to take up so much room, Vlad more than most. He swallowed up space, but he wasn't trying to dominate her. "And for the record, if he never gets his wolf back, I will support you or Arlo for alpha, so you don't have to worry about my bloody loyalty."

"Thanks, Vlad. That means a lot, but let's hope it doesn't come to that. This situation has escalated rapidly, and now that the witches and Maggie are involved, it means we have help. We just need to narrow down the search area."

"What about the rest of the pack? Some of them will have heard about the overnight attacks, and they'll be scared, too. Arlo will need to talk to them—soon. But they'll want to see Maverick eventually."

As the Pack Second it was Arlo's responsibility to liaise with the pack in Maverick's absence. "He'll deal with it. We can say that Maverick is working with a dedicated team already. That is true!"

"But how do we keep the pack safe?"

"Short of telling them to stay home and lock their doors? There's not much else."

Vlad nodded, resigned. "The wards on this place might help, but if they—whoever the hell *they* are—has Maverick's wolf, they might not work."

"You know, that's an interesting suggestion. Targeting any paranormal venue is a good way of attacking lots of us at once. So why didn't they?"

"We would have overwhelmed them."

"Would we? With no defences? Unlikely, if just one touch is enough..." Domino was getting a headache just thinking about it all.

Her wolf, already on edge, responded, uncurling within her, ready to attack. It longed to howl with frustration, and it wanted blood. *She wanted blood.*

Vlad stood, holding his hand out to pull her to her feet. "Your wolf is stirring. Let's head back to the office and make some plans."

Five

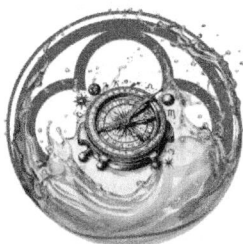

B irdie was in the tower spell room that was warded with plenty of magic for protection.

They had several towers at Moonfell, but only one designed for rituals. It was a large, round space with tall, arched Gothic windows set into the walls. A huge pentagram had been scored into the stone floor, fine metals worked into it, and the walls and doors were inscribed with runes and sigils. A bookcase contained a few books about ritual magic and other arcane esoterica, and a small fireplace allowed for the use of fire if needed. The place sang with the magic that had soaked in over centuries of use. To be honest, everything in Moonfell was soaked with magic, but this room more than most.

Birdie had carried a few supplies with her, including her staff that she used to focus her power, but most importantly she had brought the swab of Maverick's blood from his shoulder wound that hopefully contained cells of the creature that attacked him. This was a bad business, and in all the years that she had been at Moonfell, even before being High Priestess, she had never heard of such a thing. There were myths about creatures that could steal powers, of course. The one that sprang to mind was the Skinwalkers of the Navajo tradition. They could take the shape of any animal whose pelt they wore, and could steal memories, not just power. They would be unlikely, though, considering the specificity of the area, and the fact that Maverick's pelt had not been stolen.

Thank the Gods.

There were other European myths she had checked before heading to the tower. The Germanic *Nachzehrer*, for example, could steal the lifeforce from family members and take on different forms. According to what she had read, they were often former magic practitioners who turned to dark magic, and they required ritual components from victims to gain their powers. The other myth that had caught her interest was the Slavic *Koschei*, who could also steal others' powers, but needed skin or hair. However, they could also steal magical abilities. If one of her granddaughters had been attacked, Birdie would have been devastated. As for herself, she would have felt just as Maverick described. Scooped out and hollow. She couldn't contemplate life without her power. And yet she would have to, as would Maverick if they couldn't find the thief.

Maverick's ability to heal quickly had already been impacted by the attack because it was a trait of his wolf, and that had gone. His despair was almost palpable, although he was trying hard to hide it. She knew him well now, after the pack and the coven had become close over recent months, and the shock of his attack had made her realise that she considered him like family. Banishing memories of his distraught emotional state, she focussed on settling her own racing thoughts, then sealed the room, activating the wards and runes so that if any essence of the creature was revealed, it would not contaminate Moonfell. The trouble with magic was that you couldn't always predict the outcome.

She readied her herbs on a small table that she moved to the centre of the pentagram, and placing a silver bowl she had taken from one of the shelves, placed the blood-soaked gauze into it. Then she lit a stick of incense, filled a chalice with water, a bowl with salt, and lit a black candle, placing the objects in the four corners. *Now to find out where the creature was hiding*. London was huge, and to even narrow the area a little would be of great help. She had already tried using a map and a locator spell, burning a little of the gauze so that the smoke could direct them, but had little success. It had only indicated London in general, so she had decided to try another way.

With a word of command, Birdie cast a veil over the windows to dim the room, lit candles around the pentagram, then added the herbs for clarity and truth seeking to the gauze and set it ablaze; smoke curled lazily above the flames, mixing with the smoke from the incense. It was time to summon the elements. "By earth below and air above, by fire's rage and water's love, north or south, by east or west, guide us on our righteous quest. Through forest deep or mountain high, show me where our quarry lies."

The room had been utterly still, but now a gentle breeze sprang up, ruffling Birdie's hair. The smoke spiralled upwards, drawing the candle flames with it. The power in the room was charging, but so far nothing of the attacker's location was revealed. She had hoped the spell would show her the creature's location in flames or smoke, and it might yet if she enhanced the spell further.

Her magic filled the room as she said, "By earth that shakes and storm winds howl, by raging flame and ocean's growl, through realms of darkness, realms of light, I hunt thee down with magic's might. No shadow deep enough to hide, no realm where thou may safely bide. Expose the thief that veils my eyes!"

The smouldering gauze in the silver bowl twitched and then rose into the air, turning slowly before Birdie's sharp-eyed stare.

"I command you!" she cried out, her voice cracking like a whip as she smacked her staff onto the stone floor. "By earth that splits and tempests tear, by blazing wrath and floods of fear, through void upon void and burning space, we track thee to thy hiding place. No force can shield, no ward can bind, our vengeance will your body find."

The gauze burst into flames, which magnified in the swirling air, forming shapes that twisted and vanished before a true form could be discerned. It was resisting her. *Perhaps it liked the darkness too much. Maybe that's why it had attacked at night.*

"Under the bright summer sun, I command you to reveal your darkest lair."

Birdie cast her hands wide, ripping aside the veil that had dimmed the sunlight, letting it flood into the room.

An almighty shriek pierced the air, and the flames dived into the chalice of water, dowsing themselves in it. The water suddenly multiplied, bubbling over like a spring and gushing onto the floor. Birdie rapidly retreated, throwing up another wall of protection around her as the water continued to pour, now more like a fountain than a spring, forming a shallow pool in the centre of the floor, unable to escape the pentagram's confines.

Interesting. It had sought solace in water. *Was it a water elemental of some sort?*

The flow of water reduced to a trickle, and keeping her own protection raised, Birdie advanced slowly. The water had formed a perfectly round pool a couple of metres in diameter, and even from a few steps away she could see that the water was far deeper than it should be. Its dark and inky centre showed no sign of the stone flagged floor it was resting on. *If she stepped inside it, how far would she sink, and where would it take her? To a lake? A river? A well, perhaps.*

She inhaled, trying to discern any characteristic scent that might determine its whereabouts. It was fresh water. No brackishness. No salt. But oh, so deep. The coolness of it called to her. It would be refreshing after the heat outside.

But Birdie smiled and raised her voice. "I am not so weak-willed, and I will not enter your pool. Show yourself to me—unless you fear me, of course. You probably should."

A ripple broke the still surface, and something moved in the darkness. Something sinuous. But was she seeing its true form, or a shape it had stolen? More importantly, how could she use this to find where it was?

The figure moved closer to the surface, finally revealing a twisted and contorted face that leered up at her, long hair swirling around gaunt cheeks and a sharp chin. Before Birdie could see it more clearly, it dived down, taking the water with it. In mere seconds, the pool shrank until it was the size of a dinner plate, and Birdie knew she must act quickly to secure a sample. The chalice was too far to reach, so she made a scooping motion with her hand, managing to catch a cup full of water and trapping it within a bubble of air.

She secured the water just in time. Before she could take another breath, the thief had vanished along with the pool, leaving the stone floor as dry as when she first started the spell.

Now

Maggie arrived back at the station in a flurry of excitement that was not dampened by Stan and Irving's gruff demeanour.

"What's got your goat?" she asked them, slinging her bag on her desk, and heading to the coffee machine. "No lunch?"

"Actually, we have been busy taking statements all morning!" Irving said, hitching his trousers up over his beer gut and leaning back in the chair. "But I can tell from the look on your face that you expected that."

"Not expected! Hoped. Coffee?"

Stan, tall and skinny as opposed to Irving's short and overweight self, shook his head. "If I drink any more, I'll explode. A dozen or so reports of stolen powers. All similar experiences."

"All in the southwest of London?" Maggie asked, stirring sugar and milk in her drink and taking a seat by Stan's desk.

"The Retreat had intel, then?"

"Some. Bring me up to date with what you have."

They described a mix of shifters and witches who had been attacked during the night and had been directed to them by the other police stations.

"But," Irving said, "they know of others who won't come forward. The community is angry and scared. There are a few who have said their own clans will be warding themselves somehow and going hunting. Others are planning on hiding. They're afraid it's the start of

something big. A plan to wipe out paranormal creatures and powers."
He stared at her, as serious as she'd ever seen him. "It's possible."

Maggie shook her head. "There are hundreds of possibilities, and so
far it's all speculation. Plus, there are lots of paranormals in London!
It would be impossible to wipe them all out. That's just paranoia! Any
patterns?"

"Touch is the only way powers were stolen," Irving confirmed. "No
memory loss. None that's apparent, at least. No common form that
stole their powers, either. The victims were attacked by birds—including owls, a raven, and a hawk. A couple of shadowy figures as well,
and one moth."

Maggie nearly spat her coffee out. "A *moth*?"

"According to a young witch, yes. She was convinced. Actually, that
was another pattern. Those who came to see us were young. Vulnerable. Older and more experienced paranormal community members
will take care of it themselves."

"Unless they weren't targeted," Stan suggested.

Maggie rolled her eyes. "How do you explain Maverick, then?"

"Sorry." Stan sighed. "It's been a busy morning."

"I get it. Well, I spotted a pattern as I mentioned earlier. They're in
the southwest, and Hampton Court Palace seems to be the centre of
them. Not that it helps that much. That place is huge!"

"We noticed southwest, but not the palace." Irving frowned. "Are
you sure?"

"Unless anything derails that theory, we stick with it for now. It
has extensive grounds, so our attacker could be hiding there. Can one
of you call Nahum? I think the witches have already alerted him to
the problem." Her thoughts flew to her good friend Olivia, Nahum's
pregnant partner. The thought of anything happening to either of
them enraged her. It was bad enough that Maverick had been attacked.

Maggie prided herself on remaining calm and objective, but this was suddenly feeling personal, and she didn't like it one bit. "Ask him to meet me at Moonfell. Say late afternoon. I want his help tracking this bastard down. And see if Domino and Arlo can be there, too. We need strategies."

Stan's eyes lit up. "Can we come? I want to be in on the hunt, too."

"Absolutely. The more the merrier."

"Speaking of which, any minute now you'll have a visitor." Stan cocked his head at Irving and smirked. "An interesting one. The Raven Queen."

"Holy shit!" Maggie sat upright, sloshing coffee over her lap.

Irving tossed her a tissue off his desk. "What a looker! Glossy black hair. Compelling eyes. Killer figure. Uncanny."

"I know what she fucking looks like!" Maggie cared less about her looks than why she wanted to see Maggie. They had met briefly a few months earlier, and as yet, Maggie wasn't sure what to think of her. "What does she want?"

"She wouldn't talk to us, Guv. She only wanted you." Stan tapped his watch. "She'll be here any minute."

Maggie's thoughts were so scattered, she didn't know what to think. All she knew was that she had questions. *Lots of them.* "Was she threatening?"

"We'd hardly invite her back if she was!" Stan looked outraged. "Give us some bloody credit."

"Fine. Of course."

But it wasn't fine at all. It sounded like another heap of trouble.

Six

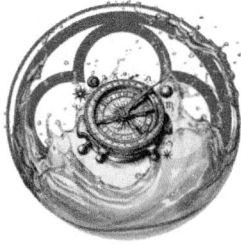

Maverick spent hours exploring Moonfell's garden on his own, contemplating his revenge on the thief that had stolen his wolf.

He may not have his usual power and strength, but he wasn't useless. He could still fight, and if the witches could paint him in sigils, it might give him some protection for what lay ahead. Plans were being formulated, and he had no intention of being left out of them.

The witches were all in the house, doing whatever magic was needed to hunt down the creature, and he was waiting impatiently for his pack to bring him news. He had only returned to the summerhouse for a short time when he was joined by Arlo and Vlad. Both were being overly deferential, and it infuriated him.

"You don't normally behave like this!" he said to them. "You're unusually polite!"

"You're the alpha," Vlad pointed out. "We're always polite."

"Not like this. You're being careful. I'm not made of glass."

Arlo huffed. "You're cranky, and we're well aware that we are stronger than you. It's freaky for us too, Mav. We're trying to do the right thing."

Maverick raked his hand through his hair, frustrated with everything. "Of course. How's the pack?"

"I initiated the alert system we set up months ago, so texted everyone to tell them to stay home. I decided a meeting at Storm Moon would not be productive and that your absence would raise questions. They know there's a threat, and that we're working on a solution."

"That was a good idea. Thank you." Maverick dropped into one of the cane chairs, and the others sat, too. "Did you say what kind of threat?

"I didn't need to." He studied Maverick, eyebrow cocked. "Did you know there had been more thefts?"

Maverick sat upright in shock. "Of shifter powers? No!"

"Rumours are spreading like wildfire. Not that the pack knows you were involved at all, of course," he added hurriedly.

"This is bad. Very bad. Fuck!"

Arlo huffed. "I received questions, of course, but I deflected all of them."

"I don't know if knowing others were attacked makes me feel better or worse. At least I wasn't singled out. Is there any other news?"

Vlad nodded. "Everyone is meeting here soon. There have been a lot of phone conversations. Maggie has been good enough to share what she had found out, and she, her sergeants, Nahum, Domino, and Grey are all coming. We're going to plan our strategy, and hopefully strike tonight."

"So soon? We have enough to go on?"

"We can't afford to wait." He related the multitude of attacks that had occurred. "There were too many in a short time. No one wants another night like that. The community is rattled."

"Plus," Arlo continued, "we're all worried that it might be a one-night event, and the creature will flee before we can take it down. Neither of those options is good."

"You think it's only one creature? Even after all the attacks?"

"It's one theory, amongst many." Arlo pulled three beers from a backpack he'd slung on the floor, popped the caps, and handed them out. "We strike, regardless. Wolves, witches, and a Nephilim should be a good combination. And the humans, of course. Grey will come, too."

"How did Grey take the news?"

"He was worried. He wants a stable pack, just like we do. He'll do what he can to help."

Grey was human, but he was quick-thinking and very capable, and also not easily intimidated by a bunch of paranormal creatures. "Good. But where are we striking? Are we just planning to roam London?"

Arlo grinned. "Maggie has narrowed down our search area. Now we just need to narrow it down even more."

NOW

The Raven Queen strode across the main room towards Maggie's office as if she owned the place.

She was of average height, slender, and dressed entirely in black. Her tanned legs were clad in stylish linen shorts, her toned arms were revealed by a silk, sleeveless shirt that shouted designer, and she wore wedged heels that made her look far taller than she was. Everything about her oozed sophistication and glamour. Her long, shiny hair had hints of blue, it was so black, and her lips were painted dark red.

Both Stan and Irving watched her from their desks, but she ignored them, eyes only on Maggie.

Maggie rose to her feet and extended her hand. "We meet again, Raven Queen. You said you were leaving London the last time we met."

She smiled, revealing perfectly white and even teeth. "I was hasty. I have decided to stay, and it's a pleasure to see you again."

Her voice had a trace of an accent that Maggie couldn't quite place. Something European. "Have a seat, please. I confess, when we first met I had no idea there was such a thing as a Raven Queen. I have heard of the Raven King, but thought he was myth."

"Not myth—merely between worlds. More spirit than flesh. I, however, am fully flesh and blood."

"So it seems." Maggie blinked, trying hard to maintain eye contact. The woman's eyes were black, with barely any white showing, and her unnerving stare was as controlling as Maverick's. "How long are you planning on staying?"

"I am establishing a base here. A home. There are many bird clans here who have welcomed me, and I will be creating..." she hesitated, "*connections*. But of course, I am aware of the situation that occurred overnight. I consider this a good time to fortify those connections, and as such I am here to offer my help to you."

Maggie wasn't sure whether this was good or bad. The woman had power and charisma, but she was an unknown quantity. "I appreciate your offer, but I work with people I know I can trust, and I don't know you at all. In fact, I rarely have dealings with any bird-shifters. Why do they even need a queen? Is there an issue here? And what the fuck is your actual name? Because I'm most certainly not going to address you as Queen!"

Her eyes danced with humour. "Maggie—may I call you that? DI Milne seems so formal. I think if we are to be on first-name terms, it should be reciprocal. My name is Calixta Darkholme of the Darkholme Clan that ruled the Aerikeen for centuries in this world until infighting and conflict meant the rule of monarchy was cast aside."

Maggie interrupted her. "The Aerikeen?"

"The ancient name of the bird-shifters. It is now resurrected, along with the monarchy. But I will leave the politics for another day. We have more pressing issues to address." Her pupils dilated until the whites completely disappeared. "A thief is amongst us. My people are affected. I need to help them."

"You're not scared of losing your own power?"

"Fear is overrated. No." She leaned forward, elbows on Maggie's desk, chin steepling on long, elegant fingers, her nails painted the same red as her lipstick. "I mean to establish myself here, therefore I must help."

"But you need my help to introduce yourself to the players in London. Some of them, at least. What have you heard?"

"I know there are two main wolf packs. I do not like Castor Pollux of the North London Pack. Maverick Hale, on the other hand, sounds far more interesting."

"You haven't met him yet?"

"He's on my to-do list." She smiled seductively, and Maggie wondered if the double entendre was deliberate. "I am planning to visit his club. Storm Moon?" Maggie nodded. "But I know that you know him, and that you will be working with him on this. Such are the rumours in our world. Correct?"

"Correct."

"Good. Then I can meet him sooner than planned and we can all work together."

Did she know that he had lost his wolf? Was this a ploy to attack? Surely not. But what did she know of this woman and her aspirations or ambitions?

"I'm working with several people on this, and none of them know you. Now is not—"

"Are any other Aerikeen working with you on this?"

"No."

"And yet flight is an advantage."

She clearly didn't know about Nahum, and it could stay that way for now. "You have a team you'd use?"

"Two others only. My closest associates. I am...assessing others."

"You make it sound as if you're building an attack force." *Surely, bad news.*

"I am forming my Inner Court. It takes time. As you said, trust is paramount."

"So, this ascension to the crown is new?"

"In a way."

Cagey. Maggie smiled and leaned back. "You need to catch the thief to prove your worth to the various clans."

"Amongst other things. But I want this city to be safe too, and I genuinely do need to make connections."

Maggie wasn't sure if she'd be a fool for turning her down or accepting her help, but she'd rather have the Raven Queen on side than as an enemy, and she really needed to find out more about her.

"Fine. Let me make some calls."

Seven

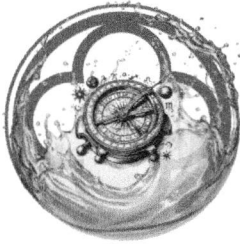

It was a very interesting group, Morgana thought, as she studied the mix of people gathered in Moonfell's library.

The three witches had been intrigued by the inclusion of the so-called Raven Queen and her two allies, and were very happy to welcome them into their home, confident that their protection spells would counter any ill-intent. Their arrival had certainly caused a stir. The Raven Queen was poised and mysterious, and the two shifters she had brought with her were equally intriguing. There was a young woman named Tyra who had ebony skin and luminous, dark eyes ringed with a tinge of amber, and a man named Alaric who she presumed was an eagle, because he certainly had the characteristics of one in human form. Tall, hawk-nosed, piercing eyes, and long fingers that looked as if they might turn into claws at any minute. They were both polite but reserved, unlike Calixta Darkholme who was calculatingly charming. Morgana suppressed a smile. *A very interesting addition to the mix of paranormals in London.*

Nahum, very dear to the witches now that they knew him well, had come alone. He towered over everyone, including the wolf-shifters, a source of controlled power that could erupt at any moment. *A force for good, though, thank the Gods.* He was originally from the Middle East, his olive skin set off by his bright blue eyes that watched everyone, especially the unknown Aerikeen as Morgana discovered they called themselves. Fortunately, Nahum had met the wolf-shifters already, although they didn't know each other well yet.

They all mingled with Maggie's team, and there was an air of tangible excitement as they caught up on each other's news, although the newcomers were treated politely but warily. Stan and Irving, typically observant police officers, were studying everyone and everything, especially Moonfell. All were eager to start tracking and fighting. *Some things never changed.*

But there was much to discuss, and Morgana turned to Maggie. "We need a plan. I presume you would like to lead?"

Maggie nodded and shouted, "All right, everyone! Let's get started. I want to catch this sneaky little fucker before things get any worse. We have a map, so gather round." She pointed at the bright red dots on the map. "These are all the attacks we know about, although we know there were even more from what we were told this morning. I'm worried we'll have mass paranoia and vigilante attacks if we don't resolve this quickly. As you can see, all of the known attacks were in the southwest of London, one of the furthest outliers being the attack on Maverick in Richmond Park."

"Just my bloody luck," he muttered.

"Maybe," Maggie suggested, "it was looking for a wolf specifically. That area is known as being one your pack frequents."

Domino frowned. "The creature wanted a mix of skills?"

"That's what it seems like. A variety of bird-shifters had their animal stolen, as well as witches losing telekinetic skills, necromancy, divination, and elemental magic. And no doubt magic to protect themselves, too."

"Which means," Nahum said, "the thief or thieves now have a range of skills at their disposal. Great."

"Anyway, the centre of that little cluster is Hampton Court Palace. I'm sure you know that it's a centuries-old palace with vast grounds, and is the perfect place to hide. However, we can't ignore that one large park sits next to it, called Bushy Park, and that Waterhouse Woodland Gardens is part of that. Vast green spaces with water, deer, trees, and therefore plenty of places to hide. There are no reported attacks like this anywhere else in the country, or in Europe, so it seems it started here. The other thing that Stan and Irving noticed is that the reports are all from young shifters or magical beings. But considering that Maverick was attacked, we think other older shifters were also attacked but haven't come forward."

"Nice work, Maggie," Grey said, shooting her an admiring glance. Grey and Maggie were a sort of couple, but Maggie was being very cagey about it all. "But can we narrow down the search area? And do we know what we're fighting yet, or even how to get the powers back?"

Morgana decided it was time to share what they had discovered. "We have had some success, but it comes with caveats," she said, adding a note of caution as they all looked excited. "I have found several spells that can aid in transfiguration, and have even found some that can steal a shifter's essence—sorry, that's the best word I can think of, short of soul—but they are long and complicated, and need far more than just touch to be successful. We might be able to use them to reverse the thefts, so I have reworked some spells we can try. What's worrying us is the vast range of powers that have been stolen. Does the thief absorb them, or keep them somewhere? I found references to objects that could contain stolen powers, and the old documents suggest that breaking that object will release the powers." She glanced at her coven. "Of course, we won't know what we'll encounter until we find them."

"Which means," Domino said, "we have to think on our feet and be versatile."

"Exactly. But we have more to share." Morgana turned to her grandmother. "Birdie?"

"I think it's a creature of water. I cast a spell in our tower room, and had an...interesting encounter. I caught a flash of its form, but it essentially made a pool in the room that then drained away. It sort of dived into the depths and took the water with it. Most peculiar." She relayed a few more details of the spell she had cast, and then held out the chalice of water sealed with magic. "This is all I could salvage."

"Water!" Maverick frowned. "So why should it care to steal my wolf?"

"Or birds?" Calixta asked.

"I don't know," Birdie admitted. "I just focussed on where to find it. Now that we suspect it's hiding in the Hampton Court Palace area, we can narrow it down together."

"How?" Calixta asked, a challenge in her eyes.

Birdie bridled at her tone. "Using magic, of course! Elemental magic. We track the water."

"Has anyone been to the palace?" Vlad asked, already scrolling on his phone. "Holy shit. It has seven hundred and fifty acres of parkland! That's huge."

"And it's a bloody enormous palace, too," Grey added. "Let's hope it's not hiding out in the plumbing."

"I went years ago," Arlo admitted, "with my mum. She loves visiting places like that. I can't remember much about it, though."

"I've been a few times," Morgana said, remembering the vast and beautiful gardens that had inspired envy, despite their own lovely grounds. "It has a huge fountain and a formal pool. That might be the source of water. There's a maze, too."

"Don't forget Bushy Park," Domino reminded them, peering at Vlad's phone as he scrolled. "That's huge, too. Looks like there's a lake in it. You said fresh water, right, Birdie?"

"I did, but the palace has fountains."

"And it's set on the Thames," Stan pointed out. "It runs along both places. That might be the source. After all, it runs through London, and isn't far from Richmond Park."

"True, but that could take the creature to any part of London," Arlo said. "And as far as we know, that hasn't happened."

Vlad manipulated his phone's screen. "Look. There's The Pond Garden and The Great Fountain Garden in the palace. That must be what you mentioned, Morgana. Those are both close to the house and should be the first places to check."

"But how do we flush it out?" Calixta asked. She might be new to the group, but she had no intention of being left out of the discussion. "And if we do, how can we secure it?"

"Magical chains?" Arlo suggested, turning to the witches. "That was effective on the demon."

"Or we just kill it," Nahum said, shrugging. "That might release everything it has stolen."

"Trust the Nephilim to suggest an execution," Vlad said, eyes narrowing.

"Ah yes, because wolf-shifters are known for their mercy," he shot back.

"A *Nephilim*?" Calixta swung around to look at Nahum, dark eyes like saucers. "I didn't know you even existed anymore."

"This is a day of surprises then, isn't it?" he said easily. Nephilim were never easily perturbed. "I didn't know Raven Queens were a thing, either."

"There is only one. Me."

"All right, settle down, you testosterone-stuffed morons," Maggie said. "I'd rather not kill it. Or them. Remember, there could be more than one. We can't cause permanent harm until we know where the stolen powers are."

Morgana thought they were all leaping ahead. "We also cannot presume it's the palace! Not yet. I know we're eager to act, but keep an open mind. The palace has lots of staff and visitors. That does not seem like a logical place to hide to me."

Maverick caught her eye. "Agreed. We need to be sure."

Odette had been quiet up until now, as was Morgana's cousin's way. Now, however, she spoke up. "I think it is just one creature, and it's ancient, from what I can discern. I saw it when I took Maverick back to the moment he was attacked. I've painted it as well as I can." She had placed a canvas on an easel and veiled it with a spell. Odette loved mischievous drama, which always amused Morgana. Now she revealed it with a flourish, earning a gasp from the group. "It's a type of Chimera—not a therian-shifter, I must stress, but something very different. The powers and creatures it has absorbed are constantly churning within it. It was hard to discern its true state at first, but the more I painted, the more I saw."

She had painted the creature with large, bold brushstrokes, savage on the canvas, bright with colour and intensity in places, but dark in others. The body was indistinct, a swirl of darkness with odd features of other animals within it, but its head was gaunt and narrow, its lips thin, peeled back to show sharp teeth.

"Well, that's an ugly fucker," Grey exclaimed. "Is it a vampire? It looks like Nosferatu."

"It has elements of that," Odette said, staring at her art thoughtfully. "It does suck powers, but through touch. I could see it as I worked. Its fingertips are pads of fine needles, designed to detect and steal many things."

Calixta stared at Odette. "That's an interesting skill you have."

"Thank you. I think so." Her lips twitched with amusement. "It means I see many things. For example, your companions are a Eurasian Owl and a Griffon Vulture. Not of your own clan. Interesting."

Startled, she said, "I'm open minded."

Morgana felt the tension ratchet. There were too many egos, and a lot of power gathering in the room. "Let's find our thief, shall we?" She tapped the map of London. "We know what it looks like, its abilities, and roughly where it is."

"Actually," Nahum pointed out, "we don't know what it looks like because it can shift, so it could look like *anything*!"

"Fair point. The shifters have an acute sense of smell, so hopefully that will help us track its lair. We can also use 'revealing' spells that will show us the creature's true form. We have tracking spells, too, particularly those useful in water, and together, we should be able to corner it. Then we can trap it using magical chains, as Arlo suggests. Then we work on the rest."

"Like getting my wolf back," Maverick said grimly.

Maggie huffed. "It's all a bit bloody vague for me, but I suppose it's the best we can do." She turned to Birdie. "Are you going to use that sample of water now? We need to confirm the right place, at least."

Birdie nodded, and started to clear the table. "Of course. We have a larger map of the area, so we'll use that."

Morgana opened the map that was part of their library collection. It wasn't new, but was good enough for their current purposes. While she unfolded it and spread it out, Odette set up the herbs and silver bowl.

"I should warn everyone," Birdie said, pouring a tiny amount of the water from the chalice into the bowl, but saving most for later, "I tried this earlier by burning a portion of the bloody gauze and following the smoke trail, but it was far too vague. Fingers crossed this will be more accurate."

Birdie dropped a pinch of the herbs into the water, passed her hand over it and cast a spell. The water shimmered and turned milky, and it seemed that the room held its breath as they all leaned in and watched. The water shimmered into a worm shape that slid over the rim of the bowl and landed on the map. Birdie continued her spell, lips muttering soundlessly as she commanded the water to reveal its source. It slid across the map, leaving a silvery sheen behind it, crossing Richmond Park and onwards. It finally halted as it entered the marked grounds of Hampton Court Palace, crossed into the Royal Paddocks, slithered past Diana Fountain, and settled over Triss's Pond that was part of the Waterhouse Woodland Gardens. There it lost its form, the worm dissolving into a splash of water that soaked the spot.

Birdie looked pleasantly surprised. "Better than I thought. That is a large area of water though, unfortunately."

"Bloody brilliant," Stan said, leaning in to examine the map.

Maggie sighed with relief. "I don't care how big the water is, we know where it should be, which means we know where to hunt. In that case, I have these to share." She upended a bag, and half a dozen unusual looking objects slid onto the table. They were metallic and ovoid, rounded to the touch so they would fit snugly in someone's palm. "Alchemical weapons. I suggest we humans carry them, but there are a couple of extras, just in case. I can show you how they work."

"Great idea, Maggie," Nahum said, striding forward and pocketing one. "I can use them, so I may as well have one." He winked at the group. "They pack a punch, so be warned. So now it's logistics. How do we get into the grounds? Is it closed at night? I can fly in, so can the birds, but the rest of you?"

Maggie shrugged. "Easy. I'll get us police clearance if necessary. We'll enter once they've closed and the staff have left, so let's say nine this evening."

Feeling uneasy, Morgana said, "It will be getting dark then. Good for it, not for us."

"We can't risk going in the light."

"We like the dark," Vlad said, a wolfish smile spreading over his face.

Maggie continued. "We have torches, and you can make witch-lights. Make your preparations, everyone, because regardless of what is happening there, we must go in tonight. I suggest we use the time we have now to study the plan of the grounds. You said we can be painted in some of your protective runes, right?" she asked, looking at the witches.

"Of course." Morgana had prepared the magical mixture. "But I should warn you that not knowing exactly what we're facing means we can't guarantee total protection."

But nothing could, and they all knew that. By the time the night ahead had finished, more than just Maverick might have lost their powers.

Eight

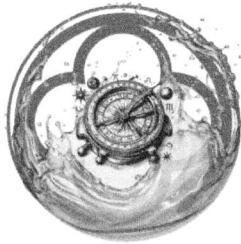

Maggie had needed to exert considerable powers of persuasion to get clearance to go into Waterhouse Woodland Garden with a *specialised taskforce*, as she'd called it, because it was part of Bushy Park, which was a royal park, and therefore very special.

Her boss had squirmed in his seat, reminding her that it was a place well loved by many, and that if the grounds or animals were damaged in any way... Maggie had pointed out that a very dangerous creature was there, and that if the staff were injured, or—heaven forbid—a member of the public, it would be a disaster. Eventually, papers were signed, and permission was granted. She should have just kept quiet and done it anyway. However, she had found out that the vehicle entrance closed at seven, so really she had no choice if they wanted to get in and out quickly.

The entrance was off Hampton Court Road, and although it was after closing, a security guard waited at the gate. She halted in her police-issued Vauxhall Vectra, accompanied by Stan and Irving, the boot filled with protective clothing and shotguns with live ammunition and salt-filled shells, just to have options. And JD's alchemical weapons, of course. The car behind her was filled with the four Storm Moon shifters and Grey, and the Moonfell Witches and Nahum were behind them. The bird-shifters, *Aerikeen*, she reminded herself, were in the final car. Fifteen of them in total, which should be plenty to hunt down one paranormal creature. *Please let the witches be right, and it was just one and not a pack...*

She leaned out of the window and flashed her ID to the guard. "DI Milne. I presume you're letting us in the grounds?"

He nodded, eyeballing the others with suspicion. "Yes, but I must remind you that—"

"I know. It's a historic place and all that." She paused, assessing the middle-aged man who had a whiff of the military about him. "Ex-Forces?"

"Yes, why?"

"Have you noticed anything odd here in the last couple of days?"

"Nothing at all, but it's been busy. Tourists have been flooding in."

"Has there been anything unusual happening here recently? Building works? Renovations?" Something must have disturbed the creature, unless it had fled from another place, looking for a new home.

He laughed, confusion flickering across his face. "There's always something happening. Why?"

"No matter. Forget I asked." She thought it was a long shot, anyway. "Seal the gate behind us, and don't let anyone in, no matter what you hear!"

His eyes slid to the group again, then back to her. "Fair enough. I'll be here when you leave."

She progressed up Chestnut Avenue, around the Diana Fountain, and a few minutes later turned left, following the signs to The Pheasantry, a café on the grounds that was the closest spot to Triss's Pond. She parked and watched the others park close by, then turned to her sergeants. "I'm still not convinced bringing bloody Calixta Darkholme was a good idea, so watch her like a hawk."

"Pun intended, Guv?" Irving smirked.

"I'm a comedic genius, Irving! As we discussed, we split into three teams, one of us in each. I have no intention of letting them run off to do their own thing. And yes, I know we can't fly, but we still monitor everything!"

She exited the car, not waiting for a reply. Although it was nine in the evening, and darkness was approaching, the heat still lay oppressive across the grounds. A shimmer of vivid shades of orange lay across the western horizon, fading to purples and then velvet dark blue, but the east was much darker. The air felt pregnant with possibilities. And danger. But it was gloriously quiet and still, and for a few moments she enjoyed the serenity of it all, knowing that it wouldn't last long.

Within minutes, those who needed them had donned their protective vests and armed themselves with weapons. Because of the heat, everyone had dressed in lightweight clothing, but the shifters and Nahum were already stripping off clothes. She had yet to see birds shift, but presumed it worked the same as wolves. They would have to strip before changing form.

Maggie orientated herself as Grey stood next to her. She had become attuned to him now. His heat. His build. She liked to keep their relationship quiet, for fear it might implode, even though she was aware that everyone knew. She feared she would jinx it. He thought she was nuts. It was endearing.

"Hard to believe that a monster is here," Grey noted, gazing around appreciatively at the manicured space around the café, and the wilderness beyond it. "I'm not much of a fan of family parks, but this is stunning."

"Henry VIII used to hunt here," Morgana said as she joined them. "He was a monster."

He laughed. "Ouch! Maybe this place breeds them."

It was wilder and bigger than Maggie had anticipated, and there was a lot of cover for a paranormal creature to hide in. It obviously didn't need to stay in water, and it struck her that this could be a disaster.

As if Grey had read her thoughts, he touched her arm gently, turning her to him. "We'll find it."

"But at what cost?"

Nahum stood alongside them, his magnificent wings of varied brown plumage unfurled, his sword in his hand. He ignored the stares, especially from the bird-shifters. He'd grown used to the effect his wings had on people. "This is a great place to fly. Sure you don't want a lift, Maggie?"

"Fuck, no! Once was enough, as you well know!"

He sniggered. "You might have changed your mind."

Domino's eyes widened with disbelief. "You flew with Nahum?"

Maggie shuffled, feeling uncomfortable. "Yes. I needed a lift up to a penthouse apartment."

"To break into it," Nahum added with a smirk. "Fun times. We found a therian."

"That almost killed me, but enough about that," Maggie insisted as everyone stopped their chatter to listen. *Not her proudest moment.*

Maverick was clearly keen to get events underway. He had a lot to lose that night. His life as the alpha hung in the balance, and he looked furious, eyes burning with determination. She had talked to him earlier, or had tried to. He was keeping all conversations short, as if he didn't want to engage with anyone too seriously without his wolf, and she hated what this had done to him. They *had* to restore his wolf. She liked Maverick, and missed his swagger, despite the number of times she complained about it.

Maverick shouldered a shotgun and one of JD's weapons. "The small pool first, then?"

She nodded. Triss's Pond was an unusual shape. It had a long tail that tapered off close to The Pheasantry, and a larger section further along. "We'll circle it. Three teams, as agreed."

They had decided there would be one police officer, one witch, one bird-shifter, and one wolf to each team, and Grey would make a fifth member for one of them. Maggie, not fully trusting Calixta, had placed her on her own team, along with Birdie, Domino, and Grey—at his insistence. He was clearly feeling protective of her, which was gratifying, but also embarrassing. Not that he cared about that. *Cocky bastard.* Nahum was to cover all three teams, and so, by his own insistence, was Maverick. His pack didn't like it, but he ignored their concerns.

Maggie turned to Birdie. "Have you brought the magical tracker we discussed?"

Birdie smiled and lifted a metal lantern with clear glass windows. Rather than a flame in the middle, though, it contained a ball of water suspended by magic. "I'm rather pleased with this. I have spelled it to glow brightly when we are near the creature." She raised it high so the others could see it. "It already has a faint glow. We're close."

"And you have spells, and—"

Birdie cut her off, a note of sternness to her tone. "Maggie, we have several spells we can use, and lots of elemental magic. We are as prepared as we can be."

Maggie took a breath, trying to be reassured by Birdie's calm words. "Good, thank you."

"The pool should be through there," Vlad said, pointing ahead through the trees, before stripping off his jeans and placing them in the boot of the car with scant regard for his nakedness, like all shifters. "Let's hunt."

Now

Maverick advanced on the narrow stretch of water ahead, a shimmer of evening twilight casting a glow on the surface.

He raised his head and inhaled, hoping to detect an unusual scent, but unfortunately his sense of smell was poor now that his wolf had been ripped from him, and the scent of verdant greenery was overwhelming. He turned to Arlo, who was close by in his wolf, a large, black-furred beast. "Anything?"

He shook his head, eyes intent on the pool, and swept around to the right. The other teams were spread out, checking the grounds as they advanced slowly. It was flat, but visibility was poor due to the trees and shrubs, and all of them knew the creature could break cover swiftly in any form. It could be watching them right now. Or had gone hunting again. He glanced across to Odette. The air shimmered around her, and he knew she was using an unveiling spell. The witches had a few at their disposal to try to unmask the creature. It might be that Odette might not even need one. She might see it anyway with her uncanny gifts. Birdie was a short distance away, the ball of water glowing faintly in the dusk.

At the edge of the pool, he looked into its clear depths. "It's shallow and there's nowhere to hide. There is bollocks-all here."

Maggie frowned. "Could the creature look like water?" she asked everyone.

Birdie cast a spell over the pool which lit up from within as if she'd activated underwater lights, revealing nothing but algae and a few fish, and then checked her lantern. "No. There's nothing here."

Satisfied, they all moved on. The larger pool was ahead, and a paved path ran close to their route, cutting through the trees and rough grass. The creature was obviously sure of itself to be so close to where humans passed every day. A few more steps brought them to a narrow channel that connected to the main pond. Maverick longed to hunt in his wolf. It was an ache so deep he thought it would break him. His pack roved around him, and Nahum and the birds swooped overhead, dipping and rising as they investigated every tree and shadowy spot. Darkness was falling swifter now, and missing his keen eyesight, he switched on his torch just as the witches released half a dozen witch-lights.

The sound of birdsong was loud as the varied flocks settled for the night, making it hard to hear anything well. Sweat slicked his palms, and he jumped as a bird broke cover, diving across the path in front of him.

Odette shouted, "Just a regular bird!"

His only consolation was that Irving had jumped too, pulling up his shotgun to take aim. They exchanged a nervy glance and progressed.

The pool appeared ahead, impossible to see fully from this angle, but many of the team drew closer.

"Fan out," Maggie instructed, "and be careful!"

It was difficult to get to the water's edge, as water plants and shrubs jostled together, and Nahum and Calixta flew in low circles over the irregularly shaped pool. Lantern held high, Birdie edged through the undergrowth, and at the water's edge, once again cast a spell, causing the water to shimmer with light. For a few moments, they all searched the depths, wary that something might leap at them. Maverick remembered the painting that Odette had done, wondering if that horrible vampire-esque face would manifest. Eddies shimmered across the surface, but nothing appeared.

"Not here, either," Birdie finally said. "Damn it."

Nahum plummeted down, landing softly. "There's a long, narrow stretch of water ahead. It might be there." He glanced at the lantern. "I think the glow is intensifying."

Maverick didn't know Nahum well, but he liked the calm, level-headed Nephilim. "Any animals close?"

"Rabbits and a few deer, but not much else. I'm pretty sure it's not them. Besides, they're moving away." He nodded to the wolves. "They scent them already."

Odette, on the far side of the pool, interrupted them, head swinging around. "It's arrived. I feel it—"

Before she'd even ended the sentence, Vlad howled and took off, hurtling around the pool to the long, narrow channel Maverick remembered seeing on the map. It served as an alarm for all of them, and the group raced after him.

Nine

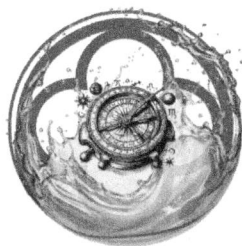

Odette threw her hands open, casting her spell far and wide, and the shimmer of magic sparkled as it sailed under the trees and through the tightly knit branches, startling the roosting birds.

Flocks erupted, causing more confusion, but in the midst of it all, she saw a dark form leap into the water. "It's in the main pool!"

The group doubled back, keeping to their three teams, and converged at various points at the top of the pool. Vlad arrived first, swiftly followed by Domino, while the bird-shifters circled overhead.

Odette hurried to Maverick's side as he shouted to his wolves, "Don't jump in!"

But he needn't have worried. They stood at the pool's edge, snarling so ferociously that Odette felt their growls rumble through her entire body.

Maverick pulled his t-shirt off and went for his boots, clearly desperate to try and catch the creature. "I'll go in."

"So you tell your wolves not to, but you will?" Grey said, incredulous. "Don't be a bloody fool! We have no idea how strong it is. You might drown."

"I'm covered in wards!"

"We all are, and we're trying to save your wolf. No point doing that if your human body is dead."

"Shush!" Maggie roared.

An uneasy silence fell, and Odette stepped closer to the edge, seeing the narrow channel of water that headed away from the top of the pool, straight as an arrow, edged closely with bushes, and contemplated their options. *The witches could flush it out with magic and then try a sleep spell on it, but if that didn't work, where could they corner it?* They certainly didn't want to kill it. This whole area was wide open green space. There was a building on the grounds not far away, but they didn't know if anyone lived there or if it was a service building. They couldn't risk going there. Or of course The Pheasantry was behind them, but that was among a sprawl of buildings.

All the loose plans they had made earlier in the library seemed useless now that she could appreciate the scale of the place. The creature had chosen a good place to hide.

"Fuck it," Stan said, eyes on the pool. "It could be at the far end by now. This is madness. Birdie, can you try again with that spell?"

The lantern was glowing a brighter blue, casting her features in an ethereal light, and she echoed Odette's concerns. "I could, but now I'm worried if I flush it out that we'll lose it again because it's so quick. We need a better plan!"

Tyra, the Eurasian Owl-shifter, flew down next to them and shifted to her human form. She was a stunning woman, her ebony skin having a lustrous glow that was magnified by the twilight. "It's a predator," she said, gaze raking their surroundings. "We need to give it prey, but we've shielded ourselves with sigils." Her large, orange-ringed eyes settled on Odette. "We made a mistake."

Odette was determined not to be defeated. "Then we need another option. It must have somewhere besides the water where it rests. We don't even know where it stores the powers it has stolen yet." She studied the dark pool again. "Unless there's something in the water. A shelter, perhaps."

"Or we're too obsessed with water."

"Or maybe," Grey said joining them, "we're being too bloody polite. Flush the damn thing out!" He aimed his shotgun at the water and fired. The report was loud in the silence, and everyone jumped. He raised his voice. "Rattle it! Get the damn thing out in the open."

Odette shouted, "No! Let us do it. We'll use magic again. Just give us a moment." She hurried to join Birdie and Morgana, aware that the hunters were getting impatient. "If Nahum flies me to the far end of the channel, and Birdie positions herself at the end of this main pool, we can cast a spell to flush it from the water. A really powerful one that will meet in the middle, herding it to where the others can wait for it, on land and in the air. Morgana, you can capture it in magical chains when it emerges."

Morgana looked uncertain, but she nodded anyway. "Let's do it."

Now

Maggie had been on many hunts before, but this had to be one of the weirdest. They didn't know what form the creature would be in, and had no sure place to corner it. She tried to convince herself that it was part of the fun.

She readied her shotgun filled with salt shells, watching the blue-white lights flushing through the water from either end like some fantastic light show, hopefully herding the creature towards them as they met in the middle. A wave of water rose as the spell progressed, sloshing over the edges of the pool. The hunting party on land were strung along the edge, gathered towards the middle section, ready to pounce, while the three birds and Nahum tracked the spell from above. The spell was designed to seal off escape on the opposite side of the pool, intending to flush it towards the waiting hunters.

Before the light was even close to them, a black shape jettisoned out of the water onto land, and immediately changed into a bird, barely visible despite the witch-lights. Birdie's lantern lit up like a beacon.

A screech split the air as Alaric, the Griffon Vulture, struck swiftly, wrestling the bird to the ground. It swiftly shifted, throwing the vulture off with surprising strength. At the same time, another dark shape bolted from the water right at Maggie's feet, tackled her to the ground, and then leapt away, leaving her with the stench of something rotten in her nose.

She rolled over, lifted her shotgun, and realised she couldn't fire because she couldn't see a damn thing. *This was a disaster.* It was dark, they were spread out, and now it seemed that there were two damned creatures to catch.

Howls erupted, sounding as if there was a whole pack of wolves, not just three of them. Grey grabbed her arm and pulled her to her feet. "This way."

A white light suddenly flooded the area ahead of her, cast by Morgana who was surprisingly quick on her feet, illuminating the three wolves, Maverick, and her officers. Just ahead of them was a bobbing figure, weaving between the trees. The wolves separated, aiming for a pincer movement, and not for the first time, Maggie wished she had paranormal speed.

"Where's the other creature? The one that Alaric tackled."

Grey pointed to the right. "That way, I think."

Before she could reply, Nahum barrelled out of the sky, sword flashing, and landed heavily on something a short distance away. Morgana was still illuminating the night, and the whole scene seemed apocalyptic. Maggie had no idea where Birdie or Odette were, and presumed that they were heading their way, but surely that would take a while. At least their sigils seemed to be protecting them. Nahum was closest, which swayed her decision, especially as Morgana was headed towards him.

"Let's see if we can secure one, at least."

Now

Morgana found Nahum wrestling on the dry grass, all limbs and feathers as he wrapped himself around the twisting creature.

Unfortunately, he was so deeply entwined that she couldn't safely cast a spell. Just as it seemed Nahum was getting the upper hand, he roared in shock and fell back, allowing the creature to spring up. In seconds, it was the shape of a man. Morgana had expected many things, but not that. She stumbled backwards, throwing a wall of protection up just in time.

The naked man was covered in tattoos, and he thrust his hands forward, sending a cascade of fiery runes towards her. She struck back, thrusting her protection spell outwards like a battering ram, and the man—or rather, the creature—countered. He spun quickly, runes and sigils tumbling from his outstretched hands, keeping everyone at bay. Or trying to.

Nahum recovered and dived at the creature, sword cutting through the air so swiftly that Morgana felt the wind of it in her face. Vlad leapt towards it, too, erupting out of the bushes, just as Irving emerged from behind the closest tree and fired his shotgun, peppering it with salt shells. The man roared and shifted, taking the form of a small bird. Alaric swooped down, grasping it effortlessly mid-flight, and gripped it tightly in his long talons, and Morgana cast a sleeping spell on it before it could transfigure again.

The bird fell limp in Alaric's claws.

"Cage it now!" Maggie yelled, racing to her.

"I've got it!" Morgana immediately constructed a cage of runes around it, working quickly and surely. "One down, one to go."

NOW

Domino raced through the grass, heedless of her own safety now that the hunt was underway.

She could smell fear in the air, and it excited her. The creature had not expected an ambush, she was sure of it. The others were with her, fanning out as they scented their prey ahead, and Arlo was pulling in front, intent on cutting it off. He howled, telling exactly where he was.

Grey was to her left, still quick on human legs, keeping up with them as she knew he would. Birdie was behind them, but she sent a blast of light ahead of them, and again the landscape lit up with an unearthly glow, throwing everything into sharp relief.

Especially the creature.

It shifted into a wolf. Maverick's wolf.

Maverick, who was to her right, yelled in shock. "Don't you fucking dare, you bastard. That's *my* wolf!"

Calixta had been flying high, out of sight until now, but her huge raven swooped down, diving at the wolf's eyes. Tyra, the predatory owl, followed suit, and the creature snapped and turned, howling as it tried to evade claws and wings. But it wasn't Maverick's howl. It was deeper, carrying the weight of centuries. It was an odd thought, but Domino knew it. Could feel age emanating from it, along with its vindictive nature.

Unfortunately, as much as Domino wanted to attack, the fact that it was Maverick's wolf made her hesitate. *Was it doing it deliberately? Did it know? Had it absorbed Maverick's knowledge of his pack?*

The wolf reared up on hind legs that grew bulkier with muscle, and its forelegs turned into sinewy, muscular arms, too. It grabbed Calixta and flung her at Tyra, and both whirled backwards, feathers flying.

"Is that a fucking werewolf?" Grey roared.

The next events happened at bewildering speed, as clearly no one else hesitated to attack – except Maverick who looked as stunned as Domino felt. The creature's broad chest was exposed, and Grey fired at it, salt spraying everywhere. Stan followed suit, the impact knocking the creature backwards and spinning it around. Odette, unseen until now, emerged from the darkness like a wraith, hands raised while she chanted a spell. The creature rounded on her, eyes full of fire. But Arlo had hidden himself well, wedged under some bushes, and now he broke cover. He leaped at the creature's head, claws raking its shoulders, and his sheer weight and speed took them both to the ground.

As Domino sprang forward, the creature exploded into water, a wall of it surging out towards them that drenched everyone. She shook it off, racing onwards anyway, and found herself being sucked downwards as if caught in a whirlpool. Arlo floundered next, as did Odette and Stan, all caught within the powerful drag of the water, and the next thing she knew, she was plummeting headlong into watery blackness.

Ten

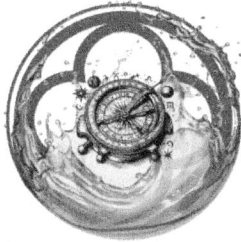

Birdie knew she had to act quickly. It was exactly as she had seen earlier.

The creature had created its own pool, and it was diving deep, pulling everyone with it.

But to where?

Maverick skidded to her side, eyes wide with horror. "They'll drown! Where is it going? And how?"

He was distraught, but Birdie had prepared for this. She both loathed and admired this creature for its dexterity and innovation, but she was determined to best it. She cast a spell, throwing all of her power into it. "By my power, waters cease! Spiral's hold, I now release. Through your centre, I cleave a way. Still your dance, my will obey."

The incessant churning and gushing of water draining into what seemed like a bottomless pit suddenly ground to a halt, and a shallow lip of water extended from the downward waterspout for a few paces in a perfect circle. Birdie hurried to its edge with Maverick, and leaning over carefully, could see a dark tunnel leading downwards made of glassy, still water. There was no bottom in sight.

Within seconds, Grey and Maggie stood next to them, and then Vlad, Morgana, the three bird-shifters, Irving, and Nahum arrived. Morgana carried a fiery rune cage containing a sleeping dove.

"What the hell happened?" Vlad asked, shifting back to human.

"An escape route," Birdie said, focussing on the tunnel again. "I have no idea if there's a pool at the base. Or a room, a cave, or even a river. Or just a void, perhaps?" She lifted her head, shifting her attention to Morgana as she tried to subdue her panic. "Regardless, Odette is down there, with Arlo, Domino, and Stan."

"And my wolf," Maverick added. He had recovered his composure. "How do we get to them?"

Calixta shifted to human, ruffled, but determined. "We can fly down."

"I can't," Nahum said. "It's too narrow for my wings, unfortunately. We need steps."

"I can make steps," Birdie said, filtering through the spells at her disposal. "But as I said, I have no idea what's down there waiting for us."

"I don't care," Maverick growled. "I'm going anyway. This is no life for me without my wolf. I either get him back, or die trying."

He looked over at Calixta. "This isn't your fight. You can leave if you want."

"Like fuck she will," Maggie said, outraged, and turned to Calixta. "You promised you'd help."

Calixta bristled, eyes flashing at Maverick. "I am no coward, and neither are Tyra or Alaric. We pledged our help, and we stay. I would challenge you for that insult, Wolf. Maybe I will when you are yourself again."

Maverick grinned for the first time in hours, and Birdie could have kissed her for calling him a wolf. It was just what he needed.

"Yeah, yeah," Grey huffed. "We do need stairs, though. I'm not jumping in blindly!"

"As you wish." Birdie summoned her power, drawing on the elemental forces around her. "Wall of water, hear my plea, form the steps for all to see. Liquid stair, both firm and true, hold your shape 'til we pass through."

With a shimmering ripple, stairs formed at the top and descended downwards in a spiral.

Maverick stepped forward. "Me first."

Now

Maverick led the descent, witch-lights illuminating the sheer wall of water and shallow, glassy steps beneath his feet.

Shapes moved within the column of water, but he decided he didn't need to know what they were. He needed to get to the bottom. It was an unnerving experience, and despite having every faith in Birdie's magic, he also suspected the creature was leading them into a trap. If Birdie's magic was temporary, they would all drown.

Shoving his fears aside, he progressed ever downwards. The descent seemed to take hours, but no doubt was only a few minutes. A witch-light illuminated the base, and with a sigh of relief, he carefully stepped onto a hard stone floor. A passage led in one direction only, a stream of water coursing down its side.

He followed it, aware that Birdie was hard on his heels, the others clustering behind. The tunnel was damp and mossy, the air cold, but the scent of water remained strong, and with a turn of the passage, he found out why.

A broad cave opened out before him, a pool in its centre fed by many streams tumbling down the walls. Lush ferns grew in crevices and in between the piles of rocks that littered the ground, and a soft, golden light emanated from an unknown source.

If he had happened upon it accidentally, above ground, he would have considered it a magical grotto. However, his attention was drawn to the four unmoving figures of his friends who were clustered on the far side of the pool—Arlo, Odette, Stan, and Domino. A peculiar looking creature stood guard in front of them. It was tall and gaunt, its face sharp and angular, its body a twisting confusion of animalistic properties and human limbs. A mess, like Frankenstein's grotesque monster come to life. Its long arms ended in giant hands, and even from across the pool, Maverick could see the tiny needles on the tips of its fingers.

"If you have killed them…" he threatened, rage building as the team entered and fanned out.

The creature raised a clawed hand, and its rasping voice echoed across the chamber. "They are not dead. Yet. But you have something that belongs to me."

Ignoring the shivers that raced down his spine, Maverick advanced. "And you have something of mine."

Birdie laid a hand on Maverick's arm and pulled him back, simultaneously gesturing to Morgana. "You mean this?" Morgana raised the rune cage containing the unconscious bird. "It's alive. For now. But that depends on what you do next. Release our friends."

The creature hissed. "Release mine first."

"I have questions." Maggie said. "You have acquired many powers over the last twenty-four hours. Why?"

"It is what I do."

"That's a shit answer."

"Maggie, forget about why," Maverick said, voice low. He studied the room as he talked, noting there was no other way out, except perhaps in the water. There was every chance the creature would dive in and suck them all down with it again, and fuck knows where that would lead. He could also see a flicker of movement from the captured team members, and didn't want the creature to spot it. "Just get this done."

Morgana edged forward to the ground on the right of the pool, holding the rune cage high. "I am prepared to leave this here. In exchange, you must release the four people behind you, and every power you have stolen. Only then will I release my magic."

The creature lumbered forward, no longer as agile as it had been, and the water rippled and churned as it advanced. "I need them."

"Then you need to make a choice as to what you need most." Morgana's voice was like ice as she held the cage high. "This, or them. Say the wrong thing and I'll destroy it right now."

Maverick had never felt fear like this. His wolf was tantalisingly close, and yet so far away. The creature hesitated, a calculating expression in its eyes, and then threw caution to the wind. It leapt at Morgana, and the water rose beneath it as if sucked up in its wake, a wall of water ready to crush them all.

Vlad responded the quickest. His wolf sprang up, and his sharp teeth bit deeply into the creature's arm as it reached for Morgana. He dragged it to the ground, causing the wave to collapse with a huge splash. The birds attacked as Nahum extended his own wings and launched at the creature, shouting, "Get out of my way, everyone!"

In the shock of the attack, the rune cage fell from Morgana's hand and into the pool. The water exploded around it as if a bomb had gone off. Grey, Irving, and Maggie ran around the pool toward their teammates. Maverick raced to help Morgana, who was stumbling dangerously close to the pool.

Nahum and the creature were engaged in deadly combat, but Nahum had the upper hand. He wielded his sword with deadly dexterity, and his wings gave him leverage. Maverick suspected that something had changed the balance in his favour, and presumed it must be the cage that had fallen in the water. But the water in the pool was getting wilder, so he pulled Morgana back to the entrance, gathering Birdie along the way, and satisfied they were out of immediate danger, ran to help the others.

Fortunately, Nahum's fight didn't last long. With a decisive swing of his mighty sword, he decapitated the creature, and its head rolled along the ground and fell into the pool, too.

An enormous, clanging bell resounded around them, like a death knell.

Now

Maggie was convinced they were all going to die.

As soon as the creature's head rolled into the pool, the water exploded again, bubbling upwards and overflowing, and the streams that flowed down the wall turned into torrents. She could barely think straight as the tolling bell became louder and louder.

"We have to get to the entrance!" she shouted, still trying to rouse Domino. "Birdie. Can you keep the water at bay?"

"I'll try," she yelled back. "Be quick!"

Maggie muttered under her breath. "Like I'm not fucking trying!" She struggled to get Domino to her feet, and with relief, saw her eyes flicker. "Domino! Wake up!"

But weirder things were happening. Shapes, or rather essences, were emerging from the pool. Shadowy, insubstantial things that churned and fluttered, and then in a streaming mass, headed to the cave exit. All except for one. The shape of an enormous wolf barrelled into Maverick, knocking him on his back, and sending Stan, who he had been helping, sprawling.

Grey, who was closest and was supporting Arlo, yelled, "Maverick!"

In seconds, Maverick bounded to his feet, and his swagger was back, as was the molten yellow fire in his eyes that announced his wolf was back where he belonged. Despite the circumstances, Maggie grinned with relief. But then it quickly faded as she saw that the cave was rapidly filling with water. The air felt thick, and the many essences the creature had stolen continued to rise like steam from a boiling pot.

"Out, now!" Birdie commanded.

They all headed for the exit, others now helping the stunned four who had been sucked down to the cave. Maggie's heart pounded, and she struggled to breathe deeply. *She was going to die down here. In a dark pit, somewhere beneath the earth's surface.* Then Grey caught her eye, a determined glint in them.

No, fuck that. She was not going to die down here.

They funnelled into the passageway, sloshing through thigh-deep water, while Birdie and Morgana remained behind them as they attempted to control the water. The passage seemed longer than she remembered, but finally they stood at the bottom of the stairway, and she could just about make out a tiny glimmer of sky high above.

"Get a fucking move on," Nahum yelled. "The water is still rising!"

On shaky legs she started her ascent, but when they were almost at the top, the inevitable happened. The stairs lost their shape as water erupted below them with a roar like a dragon that resonated through every bone in her body. The ice-cold shock of it struck her, along with the bodies of her friends, and before she could take a breath, the force of the water flushed them up and out, and they were thrown onto the hard, dry ground of the park.

The crunching landing thrust the last of the air from her lungs, and winded, she wiped the water from her eyes and rolled over, trying to see who else was out. And then another fear struck her.

The water.

But as fast as the water had erupted, it receded, pouring back down the hole until the top sealed shut with a chuckling gurgle leaving only smooth earth behind.

Eleven

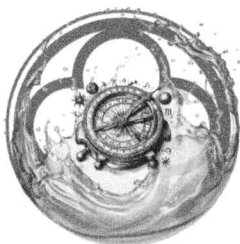

Every part of Morgana ached, but at least she still possessed all her limbs and her magic.

She stumbled to her feet, hands raised, magic poised, sweeping her surroundings for any sign of attack. But the creature was dead, the water had gone, and the bodies of her companions were strewn around her, all groaning, but still alive.

She did a quick headcount. *Fifteen of them. They had all made it out.*

Morgana felt presences all around her, and calming her breathing, she focussed on what she couldn't see: the spirits that had been stolen.

They were just as confused as she was, washed up perhaps on an unknown shoreline like flotsam and jetsam. Some of these would have come from other places, maybe even other worlds. They were all lost, and her euphoria at surviving was replaced by a feeling of hopelessness for their reunification.

A groan a short distance away caught her attention, and guilt hit her as she raced to her grandmother. "Birdie! Are you all right?"

"I am wet through, but I'm alive. Help me up!" Birdie was dishevelled, but her eyes gleamed with success. "There's life in the old bird yet, Morgana."

"I never doubted there was."

"We might need to cast some healing spells tonight, however."

"And break open another bottle of brandy."

Morgana looked for Odette, and spotted her with Arlo, helping each other to their feet. They couldn't help themselves. They just gravitated towards each other. Grey was pulling Maggie upright, and Nahum and Alaric were helping Irving and Stan. Vlad was helping a very woozy Domino, and Maverick—well, he was looking quite cocky.

Then she caught sight of Calixta with Tyra, cradling her arm, and hurried towards her. "You're hurt."

"Nothing our healer can't fix. And a good sleep, too." But Calixta's features were creased with pain.

"You can't fly?"

"It's a torn muscle."

Tyra, normally so quiet, turned her large eyes on Morgana. "Can you help?"

"Of course, but you'll have to come back to Moonfell. I think we could all do with talking it out, though, don't you think?" She smiled at them. "A chance to make connections. Helping us today, risking your life, has not gone unnoticed. Especially by us."

Calixta looked over at Birdie, and then at Odette. "You are more powerful than I expected."

"Then it's good," Morgana said, steering her toward the carpark, "that you are now considered friends."

Now

Maverick couldn't settle, even on the terrace outside Morgana's comfortable lounge on the ground floor of Moonfell. He wanted to be in his wolf again, the brief run in Bushy Park inadequate in fulfilling his needs, but that would have to wait. They had much to discuss.

Candles and soft lighting illuminated the team who lounged on the many chairs as they chatted over drinks and recovered from the hunt. Vlad and Grey refreshed glasses, while the witches moved amongst them, healing injuries where needed.

Maverick wasn't sitting, though. Instead, he stood at the edge of the terrace in a patch of darkness, watching the garden, thankful that he still had his wolf and was alpha of his pack, but movement to his left made him turn, and he found Calixta at his side. The Raven Queen was an enigma. *A beautiful one.* He had heard about her, of course, from Maggie, and had wanted to meet her, but hadn't anticipated it would be in these circumstances.

"Am I disturbing you?" she asked, her voice low and measured.

"Not at all. I'm just thinking about how much I want to run in my wolf. You fought well tonight," he told her, taking in her slender form that was stronger than it looked. "Is your arm okay?"

"It is, thank you. I fell awkwardly. Well, I was thrown across the cave, actually, and it was my shoulder that was hurt. Annoying. It will stop me from flying for a while, but Morgana's magic has already helped." She rolled her shoulder, a grimace on her face. "Give me a day or two and it will be fine. More importantly," she looked up at him, her dark, intense eyes on his, "how is your wolf?"

"As unsettled as I am." He wasn't sure he wanted to say any more to this unknown woman who would wield a great amount of power amongst her own people, and in the shifter community at large. "Once we run again, our bond will be as strong as it normally is."

"I must admit that I didn't know such a thing was possible, but I'm glad I could help. It is important to have unity in our community, don't you think?"

"Of course. So you're staying in London, then? Because it seemed you wouldn't a few months ago, from what Maggie told me."

"Things have changed."

He smiled. "You're as cagey as I am."

"For now." She looked behind them. "Your pack and my clan are talking, so that's good news."

Domino was talking to Tyra, the owl, and Arlo was talking to Alaric. "You're welcome to come by the club. It's a good place to find many members of the paranormal community. And we have great bands on, too. Are you staying close to here?" he asked, suddenly realising he had no idea where she lived in London.

"Close enough."

He hoped she was nearby. He would like to know more about her—*in many ways*, he admitted to himself, his gaze lingering on her lips, memories of her naked body vivid in his mind. Not that he had stared, of course. It wasn't done in the shifter community. Then he dismissed the idea completely. Sleeping with Calixta would make life complicated, and he didn't do complicated.

He extended his hand, and she shook it. "Here's to getting to know you and your clan better then, Calixta. And now we should join the others. I want to know what everyone thinks we fought tonight."

She nodded. "Me, too. I hope there aren't more of them."

That unnerving thought had already crossed Maverick's mind. He found an empty seat next to Maggie, and watched Calixta cross to sit with Alaric, wondering if he was more than just a member of her Inner Court, as she called it. Maggie, however, summoned his attention. "Glad to see your swagger back, Maverick."

He ignored her goad. "I know you love it, Maggie. And it's called alpha presence, not swagger."

She smirked. "Whatever. Odette has some insight into what we fought tonight." She raised her voice to attract her attention. "Odette, are you feeling well enough to talk?"

Odette had been listening to Birdie, heads close together, but she looked over and smiled. "Brandy has helped, although I must admit, I thought I was going to drown earlier."

"So did we," Maverick said as the general chatter settled. "Can you remember anything after getting sucked into the whirlpool?"

"Not much. It happened so swiftly, and the water's pull was so strong that I had just enough wits to throw a protection spell around us and that was it. The force of the fall made me black out."

Birdie patted her arm. "But you didn't drown, and that monster didn't drain you dry, so your spell worked, along with the protective runes, of course."

"Even so." She sighed, clearly disappointed with herself.

"Stop doubting yourself!" Domino tried to reassure her. "I'm a strong swimmer, but we couldn't have fought that. He was pulling us down. Don't you remember? Because Stan does."

He nodded in agreement, hands gripping his glass of brandy. "It will give me nightmares forever. Even with your protection around us, I remember it. At least until partway down. It was terrifying. Then I blacked out, too."

Arlo nodded in agreement, but didn't speak. Maverick frowned. "You don't remember anything except when we woke you, then?"

"Not exactly." Odette adjusted her position so she could see the whole group more easily. "I roused for a while. The creature used the water to carry us into the main cave, and then it just gushed away into the pool. It was the weirdest thing. It wasn't an elemental water creature, though. I think it had absorbed so many powers in its long life that it used all of them as and when it needed. Then I passed out again. It was trying to drain my magic, but the runes held it at bay. It exhausted me, though." She shook her head, sending her dark curls tumbling around her pale face. "I don't know what its name was, but I know it was old. Ancient, in fact. Possibly as old as the Earth."

Vlad snorted. "That's comforting. Any idea why it was here?"

"No. None at all. I think it probably just surfaced as and when it needed. Or when it wanted. And there weren't two of them, either," she added. "The creature split itself in two."

Maggie looked horrified. "*Split* itself? How is that possible?"

"I don't know how, I just know it did. I saw it right at the end. When you all arrived, its attention left us. We all started to wake up. I could see the bird that Morgana had put in the rune cage—see it with my third eye, I mean. It was the same as the creature. I think it was a defensive mechanism. It certainly did not anticipate being captured. When it ended up in the pool, still in the cage...well, you saw what happened. It remained in the cage, and it had no way of releasing itself. The water was part of it, I think. Or linked to it somehow. I still don't understand it all, but I will find out. I am determined to." She turned to Nahum. "And you killed it. It did not expect to meet a Nephilim. Did you recognise it?"

Nahum shrugged, broad shoulders rippling, reminding Maverick, and no doubt all of them, of the huge wings they hid. "I have met many creatures in the past, but nothing like that. Unless it was in a different form, perhaps. Do you think there are more of them?"

"It is very rare," Birdie said, "that such things exist on their own. Let us hope, however, that we never see another again."

Maverick could feel Maggie's frustration. It was radiating off her, and her lips twitched as if desperate to release a stream of expletives. He nudged her, trying to deflect an outburst. "Maggie, not everything can always be fully resolved. Be thankful, as I am, that at least we found it quickly. We have averted a major crisis."

"True." She took a deep breath and released it slowly. "Thank you, everyone. It was an excellent collective effort."

"But," Maverick added, turning back to the witches, "what about all of those powers and shifter essences that were released? I might not have been able to see them, but I felt them. Some will find their way back to their bodies, but what about any others? We abandoned them."

Morgana exchanged a veiled look with Birdie before answering. "We will return there later and see what we can do. Some of the spells I found today might help. But that is for us to worry about," she said firmly.

Maggie huffed. "I'm not sure I agree, but I'll wait and see. How soon can we spread the word that people are safe now?"

Arlo laughed. "It's already happening. Jet knows, so the pack knows, and it will be spreading around the club as we speak. It won't close for another hour. What about you guys?" he asked, directing his question at Calixta.

"We will do the same. In fact," she checked her phone, "we should be going. Tyra and Alaric will spread the word in our clans."

"And in your court?" Maverick asked.

"That too." She gave him a fleeting smile before turning away.

It answered none of his questions. *How big was her court? How many clans did she have under her control? And why was she really in London?*

As chatter broke out again, Maggie turned to Maverick. "Intriguing, right?"

"And then some."

"I thought *you* were my biggest headache."

"A statement I know to be utter bullshit."

She raised her glass. "To future hunts, Maverick."

And, he added silently as he clinked her glass with his own, *to finding out more about the Raven Queen, Calixta Darkholme.*

NₒW

Thank you for reading Night of the Wilding. I hope you loved it. Please leave a review at Happenstance Books and Merch, or the retailer of your choice.

Newsletter

If you enjoyed this book and would like to read more of my stories, please subscribe to my newsletter at https://www.subscribepage.com

/tjgreensnewsletter. You will get two free short stories, Excalibur Rises and Jack's Encounter, and will also receive free character sheets for all of the main White Haven witches.

By staying on my mailing list you'll receive free excerpts of my new books, as well as short stories, news of giveaways, and a chance to join my launch team. I'll also be sharing information about other books in this genre you might enjoy.

Ream

I have started my own subscription service called Happenstance Book Club. I know what you're thinking! What is Ream? It's a bit like Patreon, which you may be more familiar with, and it allows you to support me and read my books before anyone else.

There is a monthly fee for this, and a few different tiers, so you can choose what tier suits you. All tiers come with plenty of other bonuses, including merchandise, but the one thing common to all is that you can read my latest books while I'm writing them – so they're a rough draft. I will post a few chapters each week, and you can read them at your leisure, as well as comment in them. You can also choose to be a follower for free.

You can comment on my books, chat about spoilers, and be part of a community. I will also post polls, character art, share rituals and spells, share the background to the myths and legends in my books, and some of my earlier books are available to read for free.

Interested? Head to Happenstance Book Club.

https://reamstories.com/happenstancebookclub

Happenstance Book Shop

I also now have a fabulous online shop called Happenstance Books where you can buy eBooks, audiobooks, and paperbacks, many bundled up at great prices, as well as fabulous merchandise. I know that you'll love it! Check it out here: https://happenstancebookshop.com/

Substack

I now write over on Substack, and my page is called Where the Witches Gather. I'd love to see you there. Substack has a wonderful community of witchy writing and seasonal celebrations. You can find me here: https://substack.com/@wherethewitchesgather

YouTube

If you love audiobooks, you can listen for free on YouTube, as I have uploaded all of my audiobooks there. Please subscribe if you do. Thank you. https://www.youtube.com/@tjgreenauthor

Please read on for a list of my other books.

Author's Note

I hope you've enjoyed this novella. I originally wrote this for a Kickstarter project called Most Wanted, which was a book with six novellas and short stories about 'most wanted' characters. It seemed a really good fit for me to set this in London with the Storm Moon Shifters and the Moonfell Witches. These characters just fit together so well!

As you've probably noticed, the timeline is set just before Litha, but I wrote it before *Wolfshot* and *Amber Moon: Secrets, Ink, and Firelight* that were set before Beltane, so that was an interesting test of my planning. It was fun to write, and I can't wait to develop the Raven Queen's character.

If you'd like to read a bit more background on the stories, please head to Where the Witches Gather on Substack. I have moved many of my blogs there from my website www.tjgreenauthor.com.

Thanks again to Fiona Jayde Media who keeps producing such fabulous covers, and thanks to Kyla Stein at Missed Period Editing for sorting out my knotty—or perhaps naughty—sentences.

I must also thank my wonderful Happenstance Book Club members, who read an unedited version of this book before anyone else. I loved hearing their feedback as I was writing it. Please join one of the tiers if you want to read early versions of my work, as well as receive other goodies!

Thanks also to my beta readers—Terri and my mother. Their reassurance as they read each new book always soothes my nerves. Also, thank you to my launch team, who give valuable feedback on typos and are happy to review upon release. It's lovely to hear from them—you know who you are! I also love hearing from all of my readers, so I welcome you to get in touch.

I encourage you to follow my Facebook page, T J Green Author, Magic, Myths, and Mystery. I post there reasonably frequently. In addition, I have a Facebook group called TJ's Inner Circle. It's a fab little group where I run giveaways and post teasers, so come and join us.

About the Author

I am a writer, a pagan, and a witch. I was born in England, in the Black Country, but moved to New Zealand in 2006. I lived near Wellington with my partner, Jase, and my cats, Sacha and Leia. However, in April 2022 we moved again! Yes, I like making my life complicated... I'm now living in the Algarve in Portugal, and loving the fabulous weather and people. When I'm not busy writing I read lots, indulge in gardening and shopping, and I love yoga.

Confession time! I'm a Star Trek geek—old and new—and love urban fantasy and detective shows. Secret passion—Columbo! My favourite Star Trek film is the Wrath of Khan, the original! Other top films—Predator, the original, and Aliens.

In a previous life I was a singer in a band, and used to do some acting with a theatre company. For more on me, check out a couple of my blog posts. I'm an old grunge queen, so you can also read about my love of that on my blog: https://tjgreenauthor.com/about-a-girl-and-what-chris-cornell-means-to-me/. For more random news, read: https://tjgreenauthor.com/read-self-published-blog-tour-thin

gs-you-probably-dont-know-about-me/. To read about my journey as a witch, check out: https://tjgreenauthor.com/leaning-into-my-witch/.

Why magic and mystery?

I've always loved the weird, the wonderful, and the inexplicable. My favourite stories are those of magic and mystery, set on the edges of the known, particularly tales of folklore, faerie, and legend—all the narratives that try to explain our reality.

The King Arthur stories are fascinating because they sit between reality and myth. They encompass real life concerns, but also cross boundaries with the world of faerie—or the Other, as I call it. There are green knights, witches, wizards, and dragons, and that's what I find particularly fascinating. They are stories that have intrigued people for generations, and like many others, I have added my own interpretation.

I love witches and magic, hence my second series set in beautiful Cornwall. There are witches, missing grimoires, supernatural threats, and ghosts, and as the series progresses, even weirder stuff happens. The spin-off, White Haven Hunters, allows me to indulge my love of alchemy, as well as other myths and legends. Think Indiana Jones meets Supernatural!

Have a poke around in my blog and you'll find all sorts of posts about my series and my characters, and quite a few book reviews.

If you'd like to follow me on social media, you'll find me here:

f facebook.com/tjgreenauthor/

P pinterest.pt/tjgreenauthor/

♪ tiktok.com/@tjgreenauthor

▶ youtube.com/@tjgreenauthor

goodreads.com/author/show/15099365.T_J_Green

instagram.com/tjgreenauthor/

bookbub.com/authors/tj-green

https://reamstories.com/happenstancebookclub

Other Books by T J Green

Rise of the King Series

A Young Adult series about a teen called Tom who is summoned to wake King Arthur. It's a fun adventure about King Arthur in the Otherworld!

Call of the King #1

The Silver Tower #2

The Cursed Sword #3

NoW

White Haven Witches

Witches, secrets, myth, and folklore, set on the Cornish coast!

Buried Magic #1

Magic Unbound #2

Magic Unleashed #3

All Hallows' Magic #4

Undying Magic #5

Crossroads Magic #6

Crown of Magic #7

Vengeful Magic #8

Chaos Magic #9

Stormcrossed Magic #10

Wyrd Magic #11

Midwinter Magic #12

Sacred Magic #13

Cinderveiled Magic #14

<u>White Haven Hunters</u>

The fun-filled spinoff to the White Haven Witches series! Featuring Fey, Nephilim, and the hunt for the occult.

Spirit of the Fallen #1

Shadow's Edge #2

Dark Star #3

Hunter's Dawn #4

Midnight Fire #5

Immortal Dusk #6

Brotherhood of the Fallen #7

<u>Storm Moon Shifters</u>
Storm Moon Rising #1
Dark Heart #2
Wolfshot #3

N of W

<u>Moonfell Witches</u>
The First Yule (Novella)
Triple Moon: Honey Gold and Wild #1
Amber Moon: Secrets, Ink and Firelight #2

Printed in Dunstable, United Kingdom

71218550R00061